C000202988

# RESTLESS

## A NOVELLA

# JAK HARRISON
# RESTLESS

## A NOVELLA

AGNES JACK PRESS

Published by Agnes Jack Press 2017

AGNES JACK PRESS

A CIP catalogue record for this book is available from the British Library

ISBN: 978-1-9998749-0-2

Book design © Rachel Lawston

*For My Mother & Father*

# CONTENTS

# Preface

## The First Anglo-Afghan War (1839-1842)

On the morning of 6<sup>th</sup> January 1842, retreat from Kabul, Afghanistan, began. Four thousand five-hundred British and native troops and twelve thousand camp followers set out for Jalalabad, ninety miles away – Akbar Khan, the rebel leader, had assured the British that their passage was safe…

Khan didn't honour his word, and only one man survived the slaughter: Dr William Brydon.

In the story that follows, I reimagine Brydon as an unnamed soldier who returns to England years later, suffering from amnesia and PTSD. What would the impact of war and ultimately survival have on his family, and the people he comes into contact with?

*Jak Harrison, 2017*

# THE OLD BAILEY

*9th June 1851*

**Hope**

If I were to tell you that I was all but dead, would you believe me? It was the truth, but no one cared about no truth, even though they jabbered about justice. Well, there weren't no justice, not around here there weren't. Kidnapper and thief they said I was – lured him away from his poor old grandma, and her grieving an' all. But I swore, as God was my witness, I didn't do it.

The Beak pulled out the kibosh and put it on his head, saying, 'You'll be hung by the neck until you're dead, and let that be a lesson.'

'You can't hang me,' I said, ''cause who'd care for the little-uns?'

But he didn't give a damn. 'Be grateful,' he said, 'that I don't hang you today instead of a week from now.'

So the little-uns would be off to the workhouse with my ma, but she'd probably be dead before me, 'specially if Pa got hold of her.

If only I'd done what I was told, this story could have had a different ending.

1

# THE DARKNESS

# 1

*Six Weeks Earlier...*

**Hope**

Mac was dead. My only real friend. Dead.

I'd fetched the strawberry iced buns, like he'd said. A birthday tea for him and me. 'Not every day you turn fifteen,' he'd said. That was Saturday last, the final time I saw him alive.

And to think: all I could dream about all week was iced buns. Now he's dead.

When I went to Mac's room that afternoon, the door was locked and I couldn't get no answer. I was afraid to tell Ma in case Pa – who in't my pa – made me entertain one of the other visitors. I was worried for Mac though – he never bolted the door – so I jimmied the lock. And there he was. Dead. His glassy eyes staring up to the heavens.

I was afraid to touch him, but when I did, he felt like stone. Flies were starting to crawl through the cracks in the window, landing on Mac's disfigured face. Mac was dressed in his soldier's uniform, his beautiful red and gold jacket neatly buttoned up to his neck. It must've taken every ounce of strength he had left. His hands lay across his stomach –

3

like he'd laid himself out for the grave. In his hands was an envelope with my name written across it, and next to my name was his son's: Henry. Beside Mac was the pocket watch he'd told me to give to Henry if anything happened to him – the watch that had travelled to the other side of the world with him – and would bond his son to his family, he'd said. I picked it up and read the engraving on the back, Mac's shadowy words in my head, helping me understand the letters, 'To my beloved son, Henry, congratulations on your commission, 18—.' Quickly I dropped it in my pocket next to the letter. Then I left the room.

Ma wouldn't fetch the peelers until Pa was home. So she shut the door and left Mac all alone.

Then Pa came home. Drunk.

Ma told him about Mac and he went crazy. Saying it was my fault. He said I'd upset Mac, otherwise why weren't I in his room? I said the door was bolted and I couldn't get no answer. He said I was a liar. Which I in't.

Finding Mac dead was upsetting enough, but Pa ransacking his belongings broke my heart. I begged him to stop, but he just pushed me out of the way.

'This could make us rich,' he said, rummaging through Mac's travelling chest. 'These must be worth a few quid.' Pa held up a bundle of letters, tied with green string. 'Hope, get here and read me these letters.'

I'd been hanging about in the doorway, not wanting to go in the room again with Mac cold as stone. 'I can't. I don't know how to…'

'Don't get lying to me, girl. Unless you want to spend a night in the cellar.' Pa stood up and looked at me, his hard Irish eyes cutting right through my skin. 'You think me and your ma haven't heard you and 'im –' he nodded towards Mac's body – 'reading together… "Not like that, Hope,"' Pa imitated Mac, '"like this…"'

'I can't… I in't sure… I only know a few words… And…' I was running out of excuses and I knew it wouldn't make no difference to Pa anyway. Pa always got what he wanted.

'I in't asking, I'm telling! Now get on with it.' He shoved the pile of Mac's letters at me.

I took the bundle and sat in the chair next to Mac's bed, placing his private letters in front of me on the table. I looked at Mac – his red pock-marked face was now the colour of sick – and I felt as though I was about to betray the only person who'd ever trusted me. 'I won't do it,' I said, getting up from the chair. 'It's not right what you're doing. Mac was good to me, and…'

Pa grabbed hold of my hair and pushed my face down on the table. 'You can read them now, or you can read them later. Either way, my girl, you'll give in…'

'I won't. Not never!' I struggled to escape, but Pa tightened his grip. I thought he'd rip my hair out from the roots.

'We'll see about that…!' he said, dragging me from Mac's room.

Ma pulled at Pa's shirt. 'Let her go, Albert, she'll read the letters. Won't you, Hope?'

Pa shoved Ma out of the way. 'She had her chance. Let's see what a night with the rats does for her tongue.'

*

'Are you sorry yet?' Pa thumped on the door at the top of the cellar steps. 'If you're sorry for lying I might let you out before the rats get *real* 'ungry.'

I heard him walk across the floor above, into the parlour, his heavy footsteps stopping directly over my head. He said something to Ma, but I couldn't hear what.

I could hear the rats scratching and gnawing at the sacks though, and was glad it was too dark to see nothing. I'd been in the cellar all night, but I still couldn't make out the shapes of rubbish that littered the mouldy, damp room.

'I'm sorry,' I shouted up through the floorboards. 'Can I come out now?' I tried to sound tough, but inside I felt sick, ashamed that I couldn't fight back, that I couldn't smash the cellar door from its hinges and run away from everything – everything 'cept my sisters that is.

Pa wasn't always like this; some days he was really kind to me. But those were the days that the little-uns suffered the most from his gibes.

'Please let her out, she's learned her lesson.' I could hear my ma in the distance, pleading for my freedom. 'I'll make sure she's punished, I promise.'

I made my way up the cellar steps and sat on the top tread with my ear pressed to the door, waiting for Pa to answer. I tried to look through the knot holes in the wood, but could only see the cold, bare wall opposite. The rats had stopped scratching an' all, as if they were waiting too. And then it came.

Ma hit the door with such force I was almost thrown down the steps.

'What's happening?' I yelled at the top of my voice. 'If you've hurt her again I'll kill you!'

'Don't make me laugh, you scrawny rat…' He thumped on the door with his huge fist. 'I'm going out! And when I get back you best be ready to talk!'

I waited, holding my breath. Then the front door slammed, and another piece of glass fell from the already shattered panes.

'I hate you!' I shouted after him, even though I knew he was gone. 'You'll never be my pa!'

Ma was crying. 'Shh,' she whispered through the door. 'You'll only make him worse. It was an accident, see…'

'Are you all right?' I placed my hands on the cellar door, my palms flat and fingers spread wide, tapping gently with my fingertips. After a few minutes, I heard my ma start to tap and I knew she'd spread her hands on the other side. We were touching each other through the thickness of the oak door. These were the only times then that Ma showed any kindness to me – when he'd beaten her bad.

I must've fallen asleep, because when Pa unbolted the door I fell through onto the cold flagstone floor. The room was pitch black. His sour breath settled on my face, telling me that his wages were spent. That meant Ma would have to send me begging again.

'Your sisters have pissed themselves… You'd better clean it up.' He staggered against the wall opposite the cellar, so I took my chance and ran past him, through the house and up the stairs to where my two little sisters slept huddled together. I felt the wadding beneath them. It was soaking wet.

I shook my sisters. 'Wake up. You've wet yourself again.'

Lily sat up, her dark, corkscrew hair hanging over her little face.

'You best sleep in my bed,' I said. *Bed!* That was a laugh – some old sacking stuffed with rags! I pulled the blanket back and lifted them out one by one. Rose clung to me, still fast asleep. The girls were cold and damp and smelt of pee. I didn't know which one was still wetting the bed 'cause they were always clinging to each other in their sleep. After I changed them I put them both into my bed and covered them up with the only dry blanket between us. There weren't enough room for me as well, so I slept on the floor, curling myself into a ball to stay warm, feeling relieved I was out of Pa's *punishment room*.

I couldn't get to sleep. All I kept thinking about was Mac; I couldn't get the picture of him out of my head. The thought of him lying there, all alone, for God knows how long. After Pa had rifled through Mac's chattels, the peelers were called – and we were all told to keep our gobs shut.

*

The next morning Ma had another bruise on her face; this time her eye was completely closed. Pa was sitting at the table, smiling like a madman and filling his face with lardy bread and fried eggs.

'Your ma must've taken a fall last night; look what she's gone an' done to 'erself,' he said, grabbing Ma's skirt and pulling her onto his lap. 'I keep telling 'er to make sure she takes a candle when she goes wandering in the night. But she won't listen.'

I wanted to ask about Mac, but Ma gave me one of her *don't say nothing* looks and got up to fill Pa's mug. 'Those girls up yet?' she asked. 'If they're quick they can finish off Pa's porridge.'

'They'll be down in a minute,' I said, pouring out the last dregs of cold tea. 'They're getting dressed.' It was a lie. I'd already helped them dress; they were waiting for *him* to leave the house.

'About time an' all. Girls their age should be helping your ma in the kitchen. Not still pissing the bed and making more work!'

'They're only little…' I said.

Pa's chair scraped across the floor as he got up. I stopped talking. I thought he was going to belt me, but he was in a cheery mood for some reason. I was safe.

'Got a kiss for a working man then, eh?' He put his arms around Ma and pulled her to him. 'Make sure you're ready when I get 'ome. And those girls better be in bed.'

Ma smiled. But I could tell she was in pain.

8

# THE PALACE OF CRYSTAL

# 2

**Hope**

I felt like a halfwit dressed up in the bird's feather and flowered hat Ma had nicked. But Pa said I'd to fit in, otherwise the game would be up. All the toffs would be wearing hats, he said, even Queen Victoria herself. It weren't the bleeding hat that was my problem though – even Pa knew that. Pa said, whatever else I did, I'd to make sure I put the note *and* the newspaper into the boy's hands. You'd think it would be easy enough, the way Pa said it. Now here I was trying my best to *fit in*, but it didn't stop them toffs from staring at me. And no matter how hard I looked I couldn't see Mac's boy anywhere. Everyone looked the same: top-hatted men, and ladies with huge skirts. The syrupy smell of ladies was worse than at home.

'Oi, miss, can I see your ticket?' A peeler blocked my way. I tried to dodge past him, praying he was speaking to someone else. 'I said, *ticket*!' He held onto my arm.

'Um, my mistress has the ticket,' I lied. 'She's over there.' I pointed to a space over his shoulder. 'I'll fetch her.' As he turned to look at where I was pointing, I dashed off in the other direction. There were thousands of people and it was hard to breath.

As I wove through the crowds, the chatter suddenly stopped. I tried to see who was talking when a woman's voice said, 'The exhibition is now open…'

The deafening sound of cheering and clapping was followed by a great surge of movement. I felt crushed. I would never find Mac's boy now. But I daren't go home until I did.

My feet started to bleed; the shoes Pa had filched were too small and my heels were rubbed raw. I'd just sat down by the crystal fountain to shove a hanky in my shoe, when the boy walked straight past me. It was definitely Mac's boy; Pa had pointed him out a few days previous, when we'd followed him home – and I'd have recognised his red hair anywhere.

'Shall we see the diamond, Nana?' the boy said.

'Yes, Henry, that would be lovely…'

'I read…'

'Lahore…' His grandma's voice faded as they walked by.

I jumped up and followed them. *Not too close*, Pa had said, *keep them in your sights and then strike when the time's right.* The boy looked taller close up, which unnerved me. What if he grabbed hold of me, then handed me over to the peelers? Pa's voice whispered in my head: *If he tries to talk, you run. If he tries to stop you, you kick him hard. If the old woman screams, you thump her one. You don't get caught. If you do, you don't come back here. Got it?* Got it!

I dropped back, so as not to draw attention to myself. The newspaper was creased and damp from my sweaty hand. I tried to straighten it out but the dirt from my palm made a dark stain across the image of the beautiful lady. So this was the boy's ma? Poor Mac, to have come so far, but never made it home to his family. The boy turned and looked at me; had I said Mac's name out loud? I looked away and pretended to be with a family close by. But I could feel his eyes on me. Why was he watching me? I hadn't done nothing, yet. I followed the family towards the refreshment area, staying as close as I dared, trying to keep an eye out which way the boy went without being spotted.

'Clear off or I'll call a constable,' said a man, picking up his little girl.

'Your sort shouldn't be allowed!' said the woman with him, marching off as if I had the blight or something. Was it so obvious that I didn't belong? As I looked around it seemed as though everyone was looking at me and whispering. I needed to get out quick. But first I needed to get rid of the damn note and paper.

I found the boy near the diamond display, which was crawling with peelers. Pa had told me that the diamond was the most highly guarded exhibit in the place, and word was, someone was going to nick it… I tried to see if anyone I knew was around who could be the thief. It seemed as if all the toffs in London were queueing to get a gander an' all. I pushed my way through the crowds, the large crinoline skirts and cologne nearly done for me, then I spied the boy's ginger hair. *If I could just squeeze through…*

'Thief! Stop, thief,' shouted someone.

I froze. Everyone turned to look at me. I didn't know why – maybe I looked guilty. So I ran. I ran because I didn't belong. I knew it, they knew it. Now I was going to get the blame for stealing – an' a thief I weren't.

Someone grabbed at my arm, knocking the newspaper and note from my hand. I couldn't stop, so I just kept on running.

'Oi, girl! Stop…' I turned to look. It was Mac's boy. Where'd he come from? I kicked off my shoes; I could run faster bare foot. Snatches of words smashed against my ears.

'What on earth…'

'The Queen's diamond…?'

'No, a pickpocket…!'

This was it; I was going to be thrown in gaol. Pa would kill me. He'd more than likely kill Ma too. As the boy closed in, I prayed. For the first time in my life, I really prayed: *Dear God, I promise to be good. I'll even go to church on Sunday. Just let me get away.*

*Crash.*

I turned again; the boy was on the floor. The peelers were holding him down; he looked hurt. I stopped – should I go back? Mac wouldn't want him hurt. Then the boy looked at me, his face redder than the rug he was lying on. So I ran – out of the glass building and into the blazing sunlight.

# THE
## *ILLUSTRATED LONDON NEWS*
# 3

**Henry**

We were queuing for the exhibit and I was telling Nana about the provenance of the Koh-I-Noor diamond, when one of the policemen shouted, 'Stop that girl!' He tried pushing through the crowd of people who were standing about staring. 'Thief! Pickpocket! Villain! Diamond!'

I started after the girl before I realised what I was doing. I could hear Mrs Banks, our housekeeper, shouting after me, and Nana calling, 'Henry, come back!' But I kept running, weaving through the crowd who were unaware what was happening. The girl was only a few feet in front of me, and the policeman, who must've got trapped by the crowd, was yards behind.

'Oi, girl. Stop!' I called after her, but she kept running, dodging through gaps in the crowd, under linked arms and through the exhibits like a gazelle. As she neared the Crystal Fountain she turned and looked at me, her huge black eyes staring, pleading for me to stop the chase. For a moment I paused. Then they were on me – two enormous men with a grip of iron.

'An accomplice, eh? Thought you'd help the girl escape, did you?' I was thrown on the floor with such force, I thought I'd never get up again. Out of the corner of my eye, I saw the girl slip out of the glass doors and disappear.

'What's this outrage?' Nana's voice carried over the tops of heads and bonnets like a clash of thunder. 'Unhand my grandson this instance!'

One of the men hauled me up by my jacket collar. 'Your grandson, ma'am? What's he doing with a thief?'

'I w-wasn't with her, I w-was trying to catch her, until you jumped on me,' I stuttered, freeing myself from his grasp.

A crowd started to gather around us, and Nana looked ready to take on the world. 'I demand an apology this instant. The humiliation…'

'Sorry, ma'am. I was sure they were a double act, see,' said the man. Then turning to face me he asked, 'Would you recognise the girl again, young man?'

'P-probably,' I said. 'She looked like she was dressed in my nana's clothes. And she had this odd hat on – like a bird's nest. She seemed frightened too.'

'And so she should be,' said the policeman. 'Wait until we get our hands on her, then she'll be frightened, mark my words.'

Mrs Banks ran up, panting like a steam train. 'Is everything all right, ma'am?'

'It will be, once these…these so-called protectors of the righteous…apologise to my grandson!'

Nana was so mad. I'd never heard her raise her voice before, let alone confront anyone outside our home. For a moment I forgot about her illness and how weak she was becoming.

'I apologise, madam. My fellow officer thought the girl might be a distraction…' The man took off his hat and bowed. 'The real prize being Her Majesty's diamond.'

'How could anyone steal the diamond, locked in that contraption of a parrot's cage?' Nana demanded. We'd seen an illustration of it in *The Times*.

'If it weren't for Mr Chubb's ingenious device, they would've succeeded,' said one of the men who'd knocked me down. Turning to the crowd, he shouted, 'It's all right; there's nothing to see here. A mistake has been made. Carry on with your day please.' As they wandered off, he said to Nana, 'I'm so sorry, ma'am—'

'Lady! Lady Mackenzie, sir…' interrupted Nana.

'Lady Mackenzie. I can't apologise enough… You can't imagine what would've happened if someone had stolen that diamond. My neck would've been on the block, not to mention my men.'

'Just as well it's highly secured then,' said Nana. 'But now we're here we may as well take a look.'

'I'd be delighted to show you,' said the plain-clothed policeman, who I guessed must've been the chief constable. 'Come with me, young man, and I'll show you.'

Nana, Mrs Banks and several other onlookers followed us back through the glistening glass building to where the diamond sat in its huge gilded cage.

'This exhibit is closed for the time being,' said another policeman, dispersing the crowd that followed us. 'Come back in an hour.'

The chief constable ordered the uniformed policemen around and they set up a barricade with rugs and blankets thrown over makeshift stands.

'Come on, young man – I'll show you how the lock works, if you're interested…'

'My grandson is very keen on how machines work, aren't you, Henry?' said Nana.

'I w-want to be an engineer, like Mr Telford,' I said. 'Or an artist like my father, he—'

Nana cut me off. 'I'm sure the constable hasn't got time to discuss professions right now, Henry.'

After several failed attempts to unlock the diamond, the chief constable decided it must've been damaged in the foiled robbery. 'I'm sorry. That wretched sneak-thief has destroyed the mechanism; I'll have to get Mr Chubb to replace it.'

'What a pity,' said Nana. 'But if you don't mind I should like to go home; I'm feeling a little light-headed.'

'Probably too much excitement,' added Mrs Banks, taking hold of Nana's arm.

As we turned to leave, one of the policemen who'd knocked me down approached Nana. 'I think you dropped this when we mistook your grandson for –' he coughed – 'a jewel thief! I'm afraid it has gotten a little creased.' He held out a newspaper and began to flatten out the crumpled pages.

'I think there's been some mistake,' said Nana, looking at the front page of the newspaper. 'We don't read the…*Illustrated London News.*' Nana reached out and held onto Mrs Banks' arm. 'It can't be…' she said, as she collapsed on the floor.

'Nana?'

I grabbed the newspaper from the policeman, a scrap of paper falling to the floor as I did so. Before I could pick it up, Mrs Banks bent down and quietly put it in her pocket.

# THE ILLUSTRATED LONDON NEWS

1ST MAY 1851

## WOMAN WANTED IN CONNECTION TO DEAD MAN

**Unidentified male – found dead last Saturday in a Whitechapel rookery. The proprietor's daughter found the unfortunate gentleman after she failed to gain entry to his room.**

Dr Collins, of the Metropolitan Police, confirmed that the deceased was between thirty-five and forty years of age and possibly well-born, due to his excellent teeth; although facially the man would be unrecognisable to any family member. There were no identifying birth marks, nor papers. The man was dressed in full military uniform that suggests he was a soldier in the 44th Foot Regiment. Readers may recall this division was slaughtered by Afghan tribesmen at the retreat from Kabul in 1842. The only personal property was a blue linen-bound sketchbook.

The constable who attended the scene said, 'It was very unpleasant to be sure. The book of drawings had some rather distressing pictures in it. But the pretty woman was drawn over and over again; I thought she might be a clue to the victim's identity.'

According to the owner of the establishment, the man had been resident for about two years. She had no knowledge of who he was or where he'd come from. 'He was always pleasant and kept himself to himself,' she said. 'We only knew him as Mac. He'd a real fondness for my daughter Hope, who nursed him.'

**If you have any information on this poor, ill-fated gentleman, please contact the editor, etc.**

# VISITORS

## 4

**Hope**

When Ma said Mac's folks were coming, and I'd better keep my mouth shut, I thought there might be trouble. If not from 'is folks, from Ma. Despite my uselessness, it looked as if Pa's blackmail note had gotten to Mac's family.

'His sort always pays,' said Ma. 'They don't want no one knowing their business, like. Best time to catch 'em, when they're grieving and mawkish.'

Thing was, even if they paid to keep Pa quiet, I knew it wouldn't be the end of it. Pa's friends were real ruthless; knew how to make the most out of a rich dead person.

I felt sorry for Mac's folk, finding out about him dying in such a manner an' all. When he came to Whitechapel two years back, he was really sick. Ma had found him lost and fevered, and brought him back to the house. 'Look after 'im, Hope,' she'd said. 'Make sure he's all right, like. We'll make sure he pays well.'

Thing was, I hadn't danced for night visitors before and I was really scared, 'specially after what some of the other girls said they did. But Pa figured I was worth more, being young and innocent, that was what he said: 'innocent and worth the sacrifice'. Now I'd be sold off to the highest bidder – like a piece of meat.

And Mac did pay well, but he didn't want nothing from me. He was really shocked when he realised what Pa had said, and 'specially when he heard I'd be sold. So when I begged him to let me stay, we came to an agreement. He said, 'If you take care of me, and fetch for me when I need it, no one needs to know. You tell your ma that I want you for myself and that I'll pay extra.' So Mac paid Ma a year or more in advance.

I felt terrible taking his money, but he insisted. And so that was what we did, him and me – we pretended. And I did my best to make him strong and healthy again, but the drink or the opium was stronger. But I'd say this – Mac was a true gentleman.

'Hope! You made sure there in't nothing left in 'is room?' Ma was yelling up the stairs. 'Only I don't want nothing turning up, *convenient*, like.'

'I checked it already, Ma.'

I had an' all. In fact, since Mac died I'd sneaked into his room lots of times. Just to sit and think about what to do, now he'd gone. I knew that Pa would show me off to the other gentlemen. 'Get them interested,' Pa said. So I hid in the cupboard in Mac's room until they'd left. Ma was pretty mad in the morning, 'cause she got it from Pa.

'If I get hold of you, you'll feel the back of my 'and, girl,' she yelled after me. So I did my best to stay out of her way.

'Check it again! I want 'is folks to think we looked after him good an' proper. They might give us a bonus, like.' I heard Ma shuffle out into the yard, and then the familiar splatter as the piss and shit from the bedpans hit the back wall. 'And put that pretty black dress on, the one with the lace and bows. Makes you look all innocent and sad, like one of them mutes they have at posh funerals.'

So I did as I was told, and went to my room at the top of the house. I unwrapped the dress, which was tied up in newspaper to keep it clean, but it was far from pretty. When I put it on, it was too tight across my chest, but I managed to force myself into it.

I hated this place; I hated the filth, the endless men and the terrible noises that came from the rooms late at night. If only Mac hadn't died.

*

I was brushing the steps down ready for Mac's folks, when a carriage pulled into the street. I weren't sure why, but I ran and hid in the alley, which ran down the side of the house. As I peered around the corner, Mac's family climbed down from the black and gold carriage.

The lady was really tall, taller than she looked at the exhibition. And she was truly elegant, even in her mourning weeds. As she stepped down from the carriage, her dress caught on the door, exposing her stockinged leg, which the footman attempted to hide. Her matching velvet coat and dress were the colour of midnight, and edged with some kind of white fur. Through her veil I could see she was quite old, so this was Mac's ma. I'd half been expecting her husband to get out an' all, so I was really surprised when the boy from the exhibition jumped down after her.

They must've been in shock, as they both stood dead still like statues, staring at the house, like they couldn't believe it. Then the boy took hold of the old lady's arm and with their heads held high they walked up the steps to the front door, as if they were entering a church or something.

I ran as fast as I could round the back alley and through the scullery into the hallway. Just as I neared the bottom of the stairs, Ma opened the front door.

'Good morning,' I heard the lady say. 'My name is Lady Eveline Mackenzie. I received this note…' She held out the piece of paper which Pa had slipped inside the newspaper. 'From yourself I believe?'

The boy hung back and kept looking behind as if to check their carriage was still waiting for them.

Ma took the note from the lady and pushed it into her apron pocket. 'I'm afraid I don't have them here…like the note says… the letters that is…. Only it's… It's Albert, he…' Ma's face went grey, like when Pa had been at her. 'But I have some of your son's belongings. We didn't tell the peelers 'cause…' Ma didn't say why, but I knew, and I guessed Mac's ma knew too. 'You'd best come in, your ladyship,' said Ma, moving to one side.

'Hmm. Thank you.' The lady put her gloved hand to her face and coughed. 'I assume you'll want money?'

'Nana? W-what's this about? said the boy, suddenly at his grandma's side.

'Nothing to worry about, Henry,' said the old lady.

Henry stared at me hard, as if it was my fault, and as if by staring he'd know the truth. I looked away.

'Sorry, Ma'am,' said Ma. 'It in't my doing. I just do as I'm told.' Ma bobbed a curtsey. 'And I'm truly sorry, like, for your loss. Truly. This way.'

As Ma led Mac's family towards the stairs she stopped at the bottom step and gave me the nod we'd rehearsed earlier; I put on my saddest face, just like she'd told me, and kept my eyes lowered.

Ma pushed me towards the old lady. 'This is my daughter, Hope,' she said, putting her arm around my shoulder, all loving an' all. 'Looked after your son; nursed him herself she did when he was sick, like, but she in't no physician, and we didn't have no money to fetch one neither.' Ma pretended to wipe a tear from her eye, and sniffed into her special handkerchief. This was my cue to start crying, which I did to perfection.

'Please don't cry,' said the lady. 'You did your best, I'm sure.' She reached out to touch my arm. I pulled back – I didn't need no one feeling sorry for me.

'That we did, ma'am. That we did,' said Ma.

'If only he'd sent a message home…' The lady dabbed at her eyes. 'Maybe he could've been saved.'

'Lord knows…' said Ma, turning towards the stairs. 'An' I 'spect you want to see his room, eh?'

'Oh. I… Yes, thank you.'

As Mac's family walked past me, I tried to see if Henry looked like his pa, but he caught me looking and stared hard back at me for some time. I knew that he must've recognised me from the exhibition, and I wondered whether he'd believed Ma's sham about Mac an' all.

As Ma and the old lady carried on up the stairs, Henry pulled off his cap and his rust-coloured hair fell over his pale eyes. 'Thank you for l-looking after my f-father,' he said, not angry at all. 'W-w-were you with him w-w-when he, you know…?'

The words stuck in his throat and I felt guilty for playing a part in deceiving him and his grandma. After all, his pa had been kindness itself to me.

'Please, mister,' I said, without considering the consequences. 'I have something of your pa's. A letter. He made me promise to give it to you, if we should ever meet. And here you are.' I didn't mention his pa's watch – that was my insurance!

'Letter? To me? W-w-where is it?' He started towards me.

22

'My ma don't know about it – if she did I'd be… I'll get it, but please go.' I looked up the stairs where Ma and the lady had already reached the middle floor. 'She mustn't know nothing about it, or…' I stopped talking; I didn't want Mac's son knowing nothing about me, or this place.

'Or w-w-what?' he said, fixing his eye on the yellow bruise on my cheek. 'Does she hit you? I could call a constable and she'll be arrested and thrown in gaol.'

A constable! I almost laughed out loud, 'cept he looked so fierce. Henry started twisting his cap over and over in his hands, his freckled face becoming almost as red as his hair.

'No. Don't worry. Please go or she'll know we've been talking. I'll bring the letter to you tomorrow. I promise.'

The boy's grandma called down the stairs, 'Henry! What are you doing? Hurry along!'

'Sorry, Nana, my bootlace came undone.' Henry turned to me. 'How do you know where I live?'

'The letter…' I said. Even though I couldn't read more than the few words Mac had showed me, I knew what addresses on letters looked like – Lord knows I'd seen plenty. And I didn't say me and Pa had been stalking him neither.

I watched Henry run up the stairs two at a time, holding onto the banister and swinging wide as he reached the first floor.

While Ma was upstairs, feigning grief, I nipped into the parlour to fetch the letter I'd hidden under the loose floorboards, but it lay on the table, discovered, the envelope torn open and covered in dirty fingerprints. Thank God I'd hidden the watch in my room. Ma must've gotten someone to read the letter for her, 'cause she couldn't read at all. The thought of Ma going through Mac's private things made me feel bad to the stomach, 'specially the letter he'd entrusted to me. And what if she'd shown Pa? They already had enough secrets to blackmail Mac's family – what with Mac's addiction. Now they knew Mac had asked me to help Henry. So I was for the drop one way or another.

Even worse, if Pa found out about Mac's watch, my chance of a better life would be over.

# THE ROOM

# 5

**Henry**

The room smelt of rotting flesh, like the river at the height of summer. I put my hand to my mouth and tried to stifle the urge to retch.

I looked at Nana. 'A-are you all right, Nana?' I said, steadying her.

'My God!' Nana stumbled back towards the door, gripping my arm as she tried to regain her balance. 'How could this happen? My beautiful son!'

'Don't w-worry, Nana,' I said, trying to hold her up. 'It'll be all right.' I tried to sound *brave and grown-up* – that was how everyone kept telling me to act about Nana's illness.

I looked around at the filthy space. A small metal bed held a stained mattress, sunk in the middle. A chamber-pot that gave off an acrid smell was shoved underneath. A deal table and chair the colour of raw sewage faced the curtained window.

I tried to imagine how my father could have ended up in a place like this. And why.

'It was the smell that gave him away,' said the landlady. 'Must've been dead days. And the flies! Lord only knows how I'll let this room again.'

'Please! The boy!' said Nana, staring at the bed.

'Sorry, Ma'am,' said the landlady. 'Only he'd told us to leave 'im alone – wouldn't even let my Hope in, he wouldn't. It wasn't until…' she broke off.

'Shall w-we go?' I said. 'There's nothing here, Nana… Nothing.' Why Nana had wanted to see the room at all puzzled me – I thought we'd only come for Father's belongings.

'Your son's personals…' said the landlady, rattling her keys. 'Besides his jacket, there's a box with some odd trinkets. In't worth nothing; I was going to throw it out. S'pose you want it?'

Nana looked at the woman, dazed.

'We didn't tell the peelers. Albert said best to keep it private. The scandal…'

'My son is dead! Of course I want his things.' Nana hung her head and wept.

The landlady turned to leave the room. 'Oh, and there's rent owing, like! Two months. I wouldn't mention it, only I've mouths to feed.'

'I'm sorry,' I said, putting my arm around Nana. 'M-my nana is upset. How much did my f-father owe?' *Father.* The word felt unfamiliar. After all, I hardly knew him.

'Five shillings! You going to pay his debt?' The landlady spat into a small spittoon, which hung from her waist. 'Well?'

'Yes, yes, w-we'll pay,' I said. 'If you would f-fetch his belongings, please.'

'Belongings!' The landlady turned and clattered down the stairs in wooden clogs, her shabby skirts dusting the soiled floor as she went.

'Come on, Nana, let's wait downstairs.' I tried to steer Nana away from the room, with its ice-cold aura and scent of death.

Nana stood solid as if she'd been turned to stone, her silence hanging in the putrid air.

'Nana? Talk to me. Please. I just need to understand.'

Silence.

The landlady returned, carrying a wooden chest no bigger than a hatbox. 'It was locked. Couldn't find a key so Albert bust it open with 'is hammer.'

'Thank you,' I said, taking the box from her, but really I wanted to thump her.

Nana took her purse and paid the woman twice what was owed, a gesture that was lost on her. Nana's blue silk embroidered pouch shone like sapphires in this pit of despair.

Nana slipped the cords of her purse shut. 'Thank you for your honesty.'

'Honesty yeah, honesty.' The landlady bit down on the two silver crowns, and I noticed her dirty fingernails were long and jagged, her teeth yellowed and chipped.

Suppressing the urge to vomit, I wondered what would bring a man to this. What would bring Father to such a place? And for two years!

'Do you know where he's buried?' I asked.

'In a pauper's grave, no doubt – you know the Cross Bones?' The landlady coughed and spat on the floor. As she turned to leave she added, 'But if you want the other stuff – 'is letters, like – you'll need more than this…'

'What letters?' I asked, looking at Nana, then at the wretched landlady. The girl had said she had *a* letter. Single.

'I see,' said Nana, composing herself. 'So now we know what this charade is about.'

'Nana?'

'Don't you worry about it, Henry. Your uncle and I will… we'll see to it.' Nana struggled to speak and looked as if she might faint away at any moment. I took her by the arm and guided her down the dark, narrow stairs, careful not to tread in the waste that lined our path.

'And my son's letters?' asked Nana as we reached the front door.

'Someone will be in touch,' said a man, appearing from behind the landlady. 'But you'll need more than ten bob if you want to save your precious son's name.' He handed Nana Father's army jacket and hat. 'The rest weren't worth keeping.'

*To whom?* I thought. *To whom?*

As we stepped out of the gloomy lodging house into the glaring sun, the fresh spring air pierced my lungs like an assassin's dart.

'Let's go home, Nana,' I said.

*

The carriage ride home with Nana was awful. Unspoken words hung between us. As the sound of horses' hooves clattered over the cobbled streets, I held onto the wooden box tightly, dreading what the contents might reveal about my father. At the same time, I hoped that the answer to my relentless question would be revealed. Why? Why had Father left me?

It was a long drive home and poor Nana looked worn out with grief. 'Did you want to see the rector?' I asked. 'If you do, I can get the driver to turn around.'

'Not today, Henry,' Nana said, folding her gloved hands in her lap.

I rested my head against the window of the cab, watching the rabble of the city going about their daily tasks.

'Nana…?' I paused. 'What are Father's letters about?'

'I don't know, Henry. Don't worry yourself about it; I shouldn't have taken you to that appalling place. I'm sorry.'

'But…'

'Not now, Henry.'

'Nana? Do you think Father remembered us?' The stench of the fish market penetrated the air, saturating the fabric of my overcoat. 'I w-was wondering, because Mrs Banks said he must've forgotten us. She said he would never have left us if…'

'I'm tired, Henry,' Nana said. 'We can talk later.'

As Nana pulled a lace handkerchief from her purse, I caught a strong scent of lily of the valley. It made me think about my beautiful mother – some vague recollection of her laughing as she tucked me into bed. How I wished she were here now.

'Nana?'

'Henry, please…!'

I carried on. 'Mrs Banks said it wasn't Father's leaving that made Mother ill, it was his not coming back. Is that true, Nana?' I knew I'd pushed too hard; I waited for her answer.

'Mrs Banks had no right to fill your head with nonsense.' Nana turned her head and stared out of the window. 'Emma was like a daughter to me, in the end…' Nana's voice was faint. 'Beautiful, sweet Emma, she never sang another note…'

'W-what do you mean, "in the end"?'

'Not now, Henry.'

As the horses trotted on through the dark, misty streets, I tried to forget the vile place where my father had been forced to live. I tried to focus my mind on my mother. Imagine becoming so ill that the doctor said you were 'dying of a broken heart' – loving someone so much that your heart was literally *broken in two*! It was hard to believe, but that was what Mrs Banks had said: Mother had gone because her heart was broken. But what did she mean by *gone*? I tried to wipe away the tears before Nana could see them. She'd say I was getting too old to cry.

I was eager to look inside Father's box of belongings, but Nana just sat there, silent as the grave, holding onto Father's military jacket. I didn't dare risk upsetting her further, so I decided to wait until we got home. As the barouche bounced along the street, a deep, dull ache grew in my chest and I struggled to breathe. In the distance, I could hear wild dogs howling into the wind and the urge to howl with them was unbearable. I'd never felt so alone in my life.

The metallic sound of the horses' steel shoes on cobbles echoed off the surrounding buildings. The rhythm made me feel sleepy and I began to doze off as the cab rocked back and forth. The events of the past week crowded in on me – everything had been normal until the article in the *Illustrated London News*…

And that girl, Hope. She was definitely the same girl from the Great Exhibition.

# BELGRAVIA

# 6

### Henry

After we arrived home from that dreadful place, my Uncle Xavier arrived for lunch. He didn't visit often, but when he did, he upset the whole household, especially Nana. I wasn't allowed to say anything – I was never allowed. It wasn't my place, Mrs Banks said. One day though...

As I entered the dining room, Nana and Xavier were arguing.

'As I said, Mother, it's about time Henry went to military school. You can't mollycoddle him forever, you know.'

'Xavier, please don't tell me how to bring up my grandson. It is because of you that his father went to Afghanistan. Rambling on about how wonderful it all was, filling his mind with rubbish, and now this...' Nana stopped mid-sentence. 'Oh, good evening, Henry. Your uncle has dropped by to...'

'S-so I s-see. Hello, Xavier.' I refused to call him uncle. 'Are you st-staying long?'

'Henry! How are you, young man?' Xavier grabbed me by the upper arms and squeezed tight. 'Yes, you definitely have some muscles coming there. I was just saying to your grandmother – you really should be in school now. I know your nana is worried about that speech problem of yours, but you can't hide forever. I've secured a place at the Royal Military College, Sandhurst – where I can keep an eye on you.'

'I don't want to go to military school. I'm h-happy h-here with Mr Jameson.' It was a mystery to me why Xavier thought being close enough for him to 'keep an eye' on me was a good thing.

'I've brought you something,' said Xavier, picking up a large covered object from the table and placing it down in front of me.

'W-what is it?' I asked.

'I thought you might like to start collecting – like your father did.'

'Collecting what?' I said, not wanting to know what the answer might be. As I took the red cloth off the object, a large blue butterfly flailed against the domed glass bell jar.

'I expect your father's equipment is still here somewhere… I could show you how to pin the specimen if you like.'

'Pin the specimen!' Had Xavier lost all his senses? Did he not know me at all?

'It was hugely expensive. You can't imagine how difficult it was to come by…'

Before Xavier could say or do anything else I lifted the glass dome and released the creature. It flew straight up to the ceiling, bumping against the gaslight.

'Henry!' cried Nana, rushing to shut off the gas.

'What have you done?' echoed Xavier.

'I don't like trapped creatures,' I said, sitting down quickly at the table. 'It's n-not n-normal. It's cruel.'

'I can't believe how irresponsible you are,' said Xavier. 'Do you think it'll last more than five minutes up there? He pointed to the butterfly as it banged against the glass shade. 'You're a fool, Henry, just like your…'

'Xavier!' shouted Nana. 'Not now!'

'Maybe it'll come back down,' said Nana, sitting at one end of the overlong table. Xavier sat at the other end, which meant I would be swinging my head from side to side for the next hour or so. But at least the subject of military school might now be dropped.

'Henry, darling,' said Nana, attempting to settle the tension, 'Mrs Banks has prepared your favourite dessert, Winifred Pudding, but you must eat the stuffed chicken and vegetables first.' She shook her serviette onto her lap.

I looked at the neat line of forks, knives and spoons. I hated having to sit and plough through endless courses. Usually Nana kept the lunch table simple, but she was obviously trying to keep Xavier happy for some reason.

'I'm not h-hungry, Nana. Please may I leave?' I thought I might be able to sneak downstairs to the kitchen and enjoy the warm lemon pudding with Mrs Banks later.

'No, Henry,' interrupted Xavier. 'A gentleman never leaves the table before a lady.' He turned to Nana. 'This is exactly what I said earlier; the boy needs to go to school. He has no manners and a weak constitution. He needs to mature!'

'Please, Xavier, haven't we had enough upset for one day?' Nana picked up her spoon and began sipping the parsnip soup.' The strong, sweet, woody scent made me feel light-headed.

'Please, Nana.'

'Very well, just this once, mind. But no supper if you leave the table now.'

I got up and left the room at once, just in case Xavier insisted I stay. As I closed the door behind me I heard them arguing again. I stayed for a few minutes and listened at the door.

'You're asking for trouble, you realise that, don't you? I really wonder sometimes what you hope to achieve by keeping the boy home.' Uncle Xavier was obviously hoping to get Nana

33

to agree with his plans. 'You pamper him too much; he will never amount to anything at this rate. In fact, maybe I ought to look at Freddie Abbott's East India Military Seminary. That would toughen him up a bit.'

'Don't you dare come into my home and tell me what to do, Xavier! You may be Henry's financial guardian for now. But when he comes of age, this house, the house in Scotland and all your father's wealth will go to Henry. You'd do well to remember that!'

Everything went quiet.

'Damn it, Mother, I'm only thinking of the boy. With his father gone, Henry needs a man to show him what's what!'

'Do you think I don't know that?' said Nana. 'But now is not the time. Henry will come to that soon enough. This problem in Whitechapel could finish us all off yet. And, what with your…how shall I put it? Money worries…'

I waited, hoping to hear more, but the chink of silver on porcelain resumed. The subject of *me* had evidently ended.

*

Although I was starving, I decided to go to my room to look in Father's wooden box. I'd tried to slip upstairs when we first arrived home, but Nana insisted I went through my arithmetic and geography lessons with Mr Jameson. It was only later I realised that perhaps she thought Xavier would try to test me or something – attempting to catch me out so he could insist I went away to school.

I ran up the stairs two at a time, almost knocking into Mrs Banks and spilling the clean laundry.

'Henry! Slow down! One of these days…'

'S-sorry, Mrs Banks.' I slowed down until she was out of sight, and then ran up the rest of the stairs, slamming the door shut as I entered my bedroom.

'Henry!' Mrs Banks' voice echoed up the stairwell. 'What have I told you about slamming doors?'

The room was cold as the fire had gone out, but the late afternoon sun was beginning to warm the window seat. I pulled a heavy oak chair from beside the fireplace and pushed it against my bedroom door handle. I didn't want to be interrupted.

Father's box was hidden under my bed. As I pulled it out, the front face of the box caught the light and I noticed some lettering carved into the wood underneath the broken lock. I ran my finger over the neatly engraved initials...

### H. W. M.

My initials! Except that they were the initials of my father, too – Henry William Mackenzie – a man I never knew.

As I opened the box, the smell of tobacco and sandalwood stirred in me something distant. What was it? It couldn't be Father because I never knew him, but something shifted inside me. I wasn't sure what I expected to find inside the box: a link to an unknown man; an unknown world; something that would reach out to me and tell me who I was?

Inside there was the faded-blue, linen-bound sketchbook mentioned in the newspaper, and kept by that awful landlady. As I lifted it from the box it fell open; there was my mother's face again, the face that we saw in the *Illustrated London News* and which had led us to the lodging house. I ran my finger across Mother's face. She really was beautiful. If only she were still here, at least I would have someone other than Nana to talk to.

As I turned the pages, my mother's image appeared again and again amongst all the drawings of slaughter and mayhem. Dead hollow eyes of horses stared out from underneath their lifeless riders. Massacred women were lying on top of their murdered children. Everyone had wounds to their heads, legs and bodies. No wonder Nana didn't want me to see Father's things. The blank, terrified faces of the little children told the horrible reality. In amongst all the misery was my mother's lovely face – smiling out, carefree. I turned the pages, over and over. More horror, punctuated with my mother's portrait. And in the middle of the sketchbook was written the word…

## AFGHANISTAN

It had been scribbled in huge capital letters. The nib of the pen had been pressed so hard it had torn through the thick paper, leaking blobs of blue ink on the other side.

I slammed the book shut. Everything was such a mess. I just wanted to be like everyone else. I didn't want to go away to school; I wanted to stay here with Nana. Why did Xavier have to come and spoil everything? And why hadn't my father come back home?

But what I really wanted, above everything else, was my mother and father back; singing and playing the pianoforte like Mrs Banks said they did before I was born. 'Happy times,' she said.

Before I was born.

Seemed like everything was perfect before I was born.

As I went to place the book back in the box, I noticed that several pages had been torn out. I opened the book again and sure enough at least four pages had been crudely removed. I searched through the box, hoping to find the missing pages, but there was nothing. Why would someone tear pages out of a sketchbook? Had my father removed them because they were too awful? Or had someone else taken them? But why? Maybe someone from that lodging house?

I put the sketchbook to one side and looked at the other objects in Father's box. There was a silver compass inscribed:

'Come home, with love Emma. 18—'. I couldn't make out the date because the case was badly damaged. There was a knife as well, encased in a leather and metal sheath. I pulled the knife in and out of its casing, turning it over and over in my hand. The hilt was engraved with the family coat of arms, and the blade covered in butterflies, peacock feathers and rambling roses. I ran my thumb along the edge – it was still sharp. There was a long-stemmed pipe, unlike any I'd seen before, some drawing pencils, and a tattered volume of Mary Shelley's *Frankenstein*. A red ribbon marked Chapter XVI – I began to read…

*Cursed, cursed creator! Why did I live? Why, in that instant, did I not extinguish the spark of existence which you had so wantonly bestowed? I know not; despair had not yet taken possession of me; my feelings were those of rage and revenge…*

I closed the book, unable to read on. It felt as if my father was trying to tell me something, something I couldn't bear to hear. As painful as it was to see the last of my father's worldly possessions before me, they connected me to a man I'd never known. Nana may have not been able to talk about her son, or look at his things, but I could, and one way or another I was going to find out about my father. My parents might be a forbidden topic in Nana's house, but I wasn't going to let that stop me from finding out the truth. Why hadn't Father come home when he'd arrived back from Afghanistan? And why'd he died alone in that pitiful place? The only person who could help me now was the girl, Hope. Why hadn't she brought the letter as promised?

I returned to the dining room to see if the butterfly had been recaptured by Xavier. I wish I hadn't – the creature was lying on the floor by the window, its wings burnt at the tips.

# THE HIDING PLACE

7

**Hope**

It was a few days later when I saw Henry across the road. I'd been emptying the scraps from the kitchen into the alley when I felt this coldness on my back, and when I turned to look, there he was, looking half terrified. He may as well have been one of those peacocks I'd seen in the park, in his mourning suit and cap, his boots so polished you could see your face in them.

I threw the bucket down and ran across the street. 'What are you doing here? If Ma sees you, we'll both be for it.' Whitechapel was busy, even for a Sunday, so it'd be easy to get lost in the crowds. I grabbed his arm and pulled him away from the house.

'I had to find you again. W-why didn't you come? You promised!' he said.

'I'm sorry, but I can't talk now. Ma will be looking for me.' I looked back towards the house to see if Ma had come out. 'I'll meet you here, after the gaslights are lit. We can talk then.' I turned to leave.

'W-where will I go? I came all this w-way to see you. I can't go back without knowing the truth.' Henry looked down and kicked the toe of his boots against the hard stone ground. 'No one will speak about my p-parents, my nana is very ill, and the doctor doesn't think she'll last more than a few days. My uncle is threatening to send me away to m-military school – he wants rid of me for some reason. I just want to know the f-facts, that's all.' Henry pushed his hands into his pockets. 'You're the only one w-who can help me. Please.' Henry sounded desperate.

'I don't see how I can help,' I said. 'Running away in't going to help nothing, and it in't going to bring your pa back neither.' I was worried that his grandma might send someone after him, and then what?

'Does anyone know you're here?' I said.

'No. I left before Nana was up,' said Henry. 'And Mrs Banks was too busy to notice.'

Then I remembered a shop a couple of streets away that had been lying empty for a while. The peelers kept a look out for trespassers, but I knew a way in. Henry would be safe enough for a day or two.

'Look, I know somewhere you can hide for a couple of days,' I said. 'But I must be mad getting involved. Come on.'

I took Henry by the hand and pulled him down a side street. His hand was soft and smooth, nothing like mine. Henry looked worried.

'Don't fret,' I said. 'I in't going to murder you or nothing.'

'D-do you think I would've come to you for h-help if I thought that?' he said. As we turned past the Nelson Inn, Henry pushed me into a doorway. 'That's m-my uncle, Xavier. W-what's he doing here?'

'That's your uncle?' I couldn't believe Henry and this man were related. 'He knows my ma and pa; I saw them talking a couple of nights after your pa was taken away. I didn't hear what they were saying, but he gave Ma some money.'

'Money!' Henry's face turned white. 'H-how much money?'

'Shh, keep your voice down – he'll hear you,' I said, shoving Henry in the ribs. 'I don't know how much. But Ma sent me out to get some of her favourite gin. So I guess it was a fair bit…'

Henry's uncle walked past us and disappeared into the Nelson, followed by a pair of Ma's regulars. 'Clear off!' I heard one of them shout, as a couple of match kids pleaded for a sale.

We hurried along the street, being careful to keep to the shadows and avoiding eye contact with the local traders. Some of Ma's girls were making their way to the docklands, eager to separate the newly arrived sailors from their cash. I pulled my shawl up over my face so they wouldn't recognise me.

'We'll have to hurry,' I said. 'If I'm gone too long, I'll be for it.'

The lodging house next door to the empty shop was always open-house – no one ever took notice of who came or went. Henry and me slipped in through the front door of the house without any trouble, and quietly ran up the four flights of stairs.

'How do we get into the shop from here?' asked Henry as we reached the top of the house.

'Through here,' I said, opening the door to the attic bedroom. 'The landlady uses this room for her *special goods*. But most of the time it's empty.'

'*Special goods?* What are they?' Henry looked confused.

'Best you don't know,' I said, trying to change the subject.

It worked.

'How w-will w-we get into the sh-shop…?' said Henry, closing the door behind us.

'Here, help me move this,' I said, trying to shift a large cupboard. 'There's a hole behind here that goes through to the shop. Been here years, it has.'

Henry helped me move the cupboard just enough for him to squeeze through.

'How w-will we get out if someone's using this room?' said Henry, looking worried. 'W-with the cupboard blocking the hole, I mean! W-what if w-we, I mean I, end up being trapped?'

'You won't be trapped, Henry, 'cause once you're through the hole and in the shop, you can get out through the shop door or window.' Didn't Henry have any gumption?

'You go in,' I said, shoving Henry forward. 'I'll try to bring some food later.'

'And the letter?'

'Oh yeah, the letter. Yeah...'

'Thank you for helping me, Hope,' said Henry, as he disappeared through the hole in the wall.

'Listen,' I said, sticking my head through after him. 'If you're lucky you might find some candles in the shop, but make sure you in't seen.' I threw Henry a book of matches.

As I pushed the cupboard back into place, I heard Henry creeping across the squeaking floorboards of the room next door.

'Try to be quiet,' I called after him. But I didn't think he heard me.

# THE DREAM

# 8

**Henry**

After Hope left I wandered around the shop exploring, not that there was much to see. I found the candles, a dirty rag-rug and an oil lamp, but no oil. On the window ledge was a Bible. I picked it up and opened the worn leather cover. Inside someone had written:

*All Good to me is lost; Evil, be thou my Good*

It reminded me of something, though I couldn't think what. Who would write such a statement in a holy book?

I pocketed the candle, took the rug and Bible back to the top room I was hiding in, and made myself as comfortable as I could. There was still some daylight filtering through the filthy window, so I started to read the Bible to relieve the boredom, but I kept thinking about Xavier. What had he been doing with Hope's mother? I was really tired and hungry, and my stomach was growling loudly. At some stage I must've drifted off and began to dream...

*My father was standing at the side of the bed. He was wearing his red jacket with gold braiding on it. I couldn't see his face but somehow I knew it was Father. He was beckoning me to follow*

42

him, but I was frightened and didn't want to.

As Father drifted towards the door I tried to reach out and touch him. I wanted him to stay. I wanted him to speak to me, to hold me, to tell me why he'd left. But he just walked through the door without turning to look at me, without speaking. I followed him down the stairs, to the kitchen. Mrs Banks was asleep in the chair by the fire. Father put his finger to his lips as if to say shush... Under the table was the wooden box I'd collected earlier from Hope's house. It looked bigger than I recalled. And it had ornate carvings of dragons and snakes on it. Father pointed at the box. He wanted me to open it, but I didn't want to. I tried to shout – I wanted Mrs Banks to wake up – but no sound came out of my mouth.

The box was on the table now; a big iron key was in my hand. Father was telling me to open it, but he wasn't speaking. His voice was in my head but I still couldn't see his face. I wanted to see his face.

'Henry, don't look inside, you won't like what you find.' Nana was standing next to me. She reached out her hand and tried to take the key from me, but I couldn't let go.

Then the key was in the lock and I could hear the cogs moving, click, click, click. I tried to stop myself – I didn't want to see inside, but Father was making me. Why was he making me? Nana was laughing, laughing like a madwoman, and she wouldn't stop. My father was covering his ears and shaking his head, but I still couldn't see his face, just a shadow.

Only it wasn't Father making me open the chest, it was Nana. Sitting on top of the box was a framed drawing of my mother, like the one in my bedroom; like the one in the newspaper. I reached out to stroke her face, but as I touched the glass, the image of Mother let out a heart-breaking scream. Pain and fear echoed around the ice-cold room. I willed Mrs Banks to wake up.

*Nana picked up the picture of my mother, and as I slowly lifted the lid of the box, a sense of panic took hold of me. I was suffocating; I needed to get away.*

*Then Nana threw Mother's picture in the box and slammed the lid shut. The awful clicking sounds of the turning key went on and on. I could hear Mother's cries from inside the box. She wouldn't stop screaming, but more frightening was the hysterical laughing of Nana.*

When I woke up I was sweating so much my hair had stuck to my head and my heart felt as if it was about to explode.

I lay there, trying to calm myself, breathing deep and slow as Nana had taught me. I hadn't had a bad dream in ages. I tried to remember what had happened in it, which was unusual; I usually couldn't wait to forget.

I remembered thinking, *this is a dream, wake up*, and trying to open my eyes and seeing bright lights, hearing Nana talking to me, saying, 'Wake up, Henry, wake up!' But I hadn't been able to move. I'd been trapped.

I sat up; it was starting to get dark and the shop was freezing cold. I tried to rationalise the dream – that was what the doctors had said I should do. So much had happened over the last few days: the newspaper article, the lodging house, and those words from *Frankenstein*, all jumbled around in my head…

*Evil. Cursed. Rage. Revenge!*

# WHITECHAPEL

# 9

### Hope

'You little madam! Where've you been?' Ma was yelling out of her bedroom window. 'I 'ave customers waiting. Want a pre-auction peek at the goods…'

'Sorry, Ma,' I said, as I ran through the open front door. The orange and clove smell of perfumed girls hit me as I ran up to Ma's room. I waited outside for a few seconds, listening to see if Ma was alone.

'Hope! Where the 'ell are you?'

'Here, Ma.' I opened the door. Ma had her back to me, looking out of the window, though how she could see through the dirt on the inside and the fog on the outside was a mystery.

'I nipped out to fetch some bread,' I lied. 'I thought you might be hungry.'

As Ma turned around I noticed her face was bashed about again. Only this time it looked like he'd tried to kill her.

'Ma! What happened? Did he do this?' I ran over to where she stood motionless and went to put my arms around her.

*Whack!* Ma cuffed me hard across the face.

'It's your fault; I told you not to say nothing to that boy.' Ma started pacing the room. 'Albert's going crazy – says he's gonna choke the life out of you when he gets 'is hands on you.'

'I didn't say nothing, I promise.'

'Don't get lying to me, girl. You're in trouble enough already. Think me and your pa didn't know about that letter? Thought you'd take the money for yourself…? You best pack your stuff and get out, for your own good! I tried to save you, Hope. But now…'

'Now, what?' I put my hand out to touch Ma's blackened eye, but she turned away.

'He says he'll bring the sale forward – it's in two days. Sorry, Hope, I can't stop it.'

'I'm not frightened, Ma.' I held my face, which was stinging like hell. 'I in't said nothing to Henry, I promise.'

''enry now, is it? 'ow do you know his name then if you didn't say nothing?'

'I—'

'Get out!' Ma turned her back to me. 'You've been nothing but trouble since that toff came here. Should've minded your own business, but no, not our Hope.'

I tried to plead with Ma, but she weren't having none of it. 'I better go then,' I said. I waited for Ma to change her mind but she never spoke.

I turned and marched out of Ma's bedroom, slamming the door behind me. I ran up to my room, trying hard not to cry. I'd show her!

Lily and Rose were playing with my china-faced doll, brushing its few strands of hair with their fingers. I didn't have the heart to take it from them. I picked up my leather satchel, which I kept next to my bed, and shoved the few precious things I owned from when I was little in it: a baby shawl what

46

now had holes in, but must've been beautiful once; a torn and creased drawing of my ma and pa – my real pa that was. I threw the bag over my shoulder and hugged the girls goodbye. I hated leaving them behind, but what could I do?

Rose started crying and held onto my skirt. 'Hope, stay.'

I pulled her off, and lifted her up to kiss, her wet cheeks pressed against my neck. 'Please don't cry, Rosie. I'll be back, I promise.' Then Lily began to wail at the top of her lungs. I couldn't bear it.

'Listen, Lily, Rose. If you both look after my china doll, I'll go and fetch some clothes for her.' I hated lying, but I had to get out before Pa came home. 'I won't be long,' I said, prising the girls' fingers from my skirt. Shutting the door on my sisters was the hardest thing I'd ever do. I hurried down the stairs without looking back, without my precious sisters. As I crept down to the scullery to pocket some food, I could hear the girls still whimpering.

'Shut that racket now, or I'll give you something to cry about,' shouted Ma from her bedroom.

Silence.

I thought about running back upstairs and taking the girls with me. But I knew it would be impossible. I needed to focus… *What do I need? Enough food to last at least a couple of days.* I opened the pantry door and looked in the meat safe. I took some cooked sausages and a scrap of ham. From under the food cover, I helped myself to some bread and cheese. Wrapping it all up in a neckerchief I found on the table, I left the house as fast as I could. I'd explain my situation to Henry. Tell him that Mac had promised to look after me, and the little-uns, and maybe Henry would be good to his pa's word.

The streets were damp and cold and the sounds of market traders selling the last of their stock was already rising above

47

the clatter of carts, dogs and crying babies. I'd miss this place in a strange way.

'Evening, Miss, how's your ma?' Alfie the fishmonger struggled past with his handcart laden with food scraps he'd sell to the locals. His leg must've been playing him up again, as his limp was worse than usual.

'Fine, Alfie. Waiting for her gin I 'spect.' I hurried on, hoping I wouldn't see anyone else. In a few days, when she'd calmed down, Ma would send her cronies looking for me. I didn't want no reports saying which way I went, particularly as Henry was involved.

Everybody had been about their business for hours already, buying and selling their small stocks of matches, flowers and cress to the posh folks on the other side of the city. I could hear Alfie calling, 'Penny...half pint of shrimps, winkles, or three oysters.'

The little kids from my street were still out begging, with barely a coat on their backs. It looked as if it was little Annie's turn to wear the shoes, but she'd be lucky if she'd get a crust of bread to see her through the day. I called her over and broke off half the bread I'd taken for me and Henry. 'Take this, but you in't seen me, right!' She grabbed the food and ran off like a wild animal. It made me think about Henry. What if he refused to help me? What then? I might be begging on the streets myself. I thought about going home and asking Pa to forgive me, but I knew it'd be pointless – either way he'd have me sold to the highest bidder. And if I was really unlucky I'd end up as a farmer's wife in one of the colonies.

I hurried through the streets as fast as I could, diving into alleyways and doors if I saw someone who might report to Pa. As I got near to the place where Henry was hiding I saw a couple of peelers hanging around, looking in the windows of the empty shop.

*Damn it!*

I hid in an alleyway and waited. After a time, the landlady of the lodging house came out and started talking to the peelers. I was just too far away to hear what was being said, but when she pointed up to the second floor of the empty shop, I knew we'd been discovered. Both Peelers marched over to the door of the shop and, after trying the handle a few times and rubbing the glass with their sleeve, they went back to the landlady. I hoped Henry was hiding well and good.

When the peelers were looking the other way I darted into another alley. Now I was close enough to hear what they were saying.

'I know I 'eard something,' said the landlady. 'I said to my Sam, "What's that noise?" But 'e's deaf as a post. "What noise?" he says, then starts snoring again. So I—'

'All right, we don't need to know the whole story. It was probably a dog or something,' said the taller peeler. 'We've got better things to do than chase after dogs, or ghosts.' He laughed and nudged the other peeler.

'That's right,' said the shorter one. 'We've got a kidnapping to investigate. Could even be a murder if that soldier's overdose isn't what it seems!'

'Murder?' said the landlady. 'And what if this might-be-murderer-kidnapper is hiding in that shop, eh? In't thought about that, 'ave ya?'

'Well, if he is,' answered the tall one, 'he must have a key, 'cause that door is bolted good and tight.'

'What if he got in another way?' said the landlady. 'I might get murdered in my sleep!' She held her hands to her throat as if to choke herself. 'Then you'd be sorry!'

It would've been quite funny if I hadn't known Henry was just a few feet away.

**49**

'All right,' said the taller one. 'Show us around the back and we'll check the doors and windows. Anything to keep the public happy.' And all three of them disappeared into the house.

# DISCOVERY

# 10

**Hope**

When I finally got into the house, Henry had hidden in a small room at the back. It was odd seeing this strange boy reduced to hiding in an empty, shadowy room. Outside a real pea-souper was beginning to settle over London.

'Shh, Henry. The peelers are outside.'

'W-what? How?'

'Just doing their rounds I 'spect. I've got you something to eat; you must be starving.' I passed Henry the food I'd pinched from Ma's pantry. 'It in't much, but it's better than nothing.'

I lit the stubby candle Henry had left on the floor and put it down between us.

'W-where were you? I thought maybe you'd gone to fetch a policeman.' Henry tore off a chunk of bread and ate greedily. 'I was convinced you w-wouldn't come back.'

'Me get the peelers? And get myself arrested? No fear,' I said.

I knew that even if I had – and I had thought about it, for his sake – it'd be me that would get locked up, accused of kidnapping or something, like that peeler had said.

'You can't stay here long,' I told him. 'Someone might catch sight of me sneaking about bringing you food and things. And we don't want to get caught by Pa's friends.'

'Did you bring the letter?' Henry asked through mouthfuls of food.

I took the crumpled letter from my dress pocket and handed it to Henry. I felt dreadful knowing what my pa planned to do to Henry's family. And Mac's watch was burning a hole in my pocket and my conscience.

Henry put down the bread, wiped his hands on his jacket and gently took the letter from me.

'Someone has opened it! Was it you?'

'No, it was someone else…' I wanted to explain, but I felt ashamed to be mixed up in it all.

Henry sat in silence, staring at the letter. The yellow glow from the candle cast huge shadows on the walls, reminding me of the shadow puppetry Ma used to play before my real pa died and *he* came.

Henry opened the letter and, taking the candle, he moved to the other side of the room. Standing with his back to me, he read in silence. In the dim candlelight that cast an outline of Henry, I could see his shoulders shaking as if he had a palsy or something. The sound of faint sniffles came from his corner of the room, reminding me of Ma after *he'd* been at her. Whatever was written in that letter had obviously upset Henry. I sat quiet, waiting, not knowing what to say to comfort him.

After what seemed like ages, Henry turned to me, wiping his face on his jacket sleeve. 'I need your help to find my mother,' he said. 'Father believes she's alive somewhere.'

'Still alive?'

'I've worked it out…'

'You sure…? Mac never said anything to me…' I wondered

whether I should tell Henry about Pa's whole rotten blackmail scheme. The letter Henry had was scandal enough, never mind the missing letters – 'specially if Henry's ma was still alive. But what if I was sent to prison as a conspirator? I couldn't take the chance… But if I wanted Henry to trust me, I'd have to tell him about his pa.

'Henry. There's something you should know,' I said, trying my best not to sound too frightening. 'It's about your pa.'

'W-what about my father?'

'Well… When he first got here, your pa that is, he was rambling a lot. He was really ailing, Henry. And at night when I stayed with him, he would talk in his sleep. Sometimes it didn't make any sense – just odd words and the like…' This was going to be harder than I thought.

'And?'

'And, he said things which might've been about your mother. I in't certain. But now you say she might be alive, it makes perfect sense.'

Henry stood up and started pacing the room like a caged lion, bombarding me with questions about Mac. Questions I didn't want to answer for fear of upsetting him; questions I couldn't answer because of my ma. If Pa's friends found out I was even talking to Henry they'd string me up.

'Did Father say anything that might tell me where Mother is? Anything? A clue maybe?' Henry took a handkerchief from inside his jacket and dabbed his eyes.

'I'm not sure. He kept saying it was his fault. He called your mother his little nightingale,' I said.

I didn't want to tell Henry about his father's night sweats and the late night screaming. I didn't want to upset Henry in any way. Yet in order to help him I would have to tell Henry everything I knew.

'Henry, your father was very ill. I don't know how much of what he said was true because he rambled a lot in his sleep. But one thing he kept saying over and over was, "They've locked my songbird away and she can't sing anymore." I didn't know what he meant. I thought he'd gone mad with the opium.'

'W-what do you mean, opium?' Henry lurched at me, his face red with anger. 'Do you know something you're not telling me?'

'No. I'm just saying, if there's any truth in what your father said, then maybe...'

I didn't finish what I was saying because Henry started to leave. 'Where are you going? It's not safe out there at night, 'specially looking like you do,' I said. 'You're a walking target.'

'I need to get home and talk to Nana,' he said, pulling his cap down over his eyes. 'I'll ask her s-straight out and if she won't t-talk then I'll find the truth some other way. If my mother *is* still alive, then I'm going to find her.'

'Listen,' I said. 'I'll show you the way home tomorrow if you want to go back. But we need to stay here tonight – I'll keep you company. I can't risk being seen anyway – Pa will be out looking for me.'

After a minute or two Henry sat down by the window and picked at his food. Once he'd finished, I shuffled onto the floor and pulled my shawl over my head, trying to block out the reality of my situation: if Henry went home to get help, then he wouldn't need me.

The room was bitterly cold and as night closed in the damp air soaked through my thin cotton dress. Outside, the dark sounds of the city gradually masked the friendlier tones of day. Another hour or two and the shrieks of local girls earning a crust would penetrate the relative quiet of the room. And if Pa got hold of me, I'd be joining them.

# THE LETTER

# 11

**Henry**

Hope stayed behind to keep me company, she said, and she did help calm me down. At first, I wanted her to go so I could read the letter again without her constantly interrupting me. But after she fell asleep, I felt so alone and the room seemed so creepy that I was glad she'd stayed. I could feel my imagination starting to get the better of me, and my heart started pounding. The passages from Mary Shelley's novel kept repeating over and over in my mind. *Cursed creature* – was that how my father felt? The reason he never returned home? I unfolded Father's letter and tried to settle down to reread it, hoping that it would help me feel close to the man I never knew – close enough for him to protect me, even if he was now in Heaven, if there was such a place. As I read – running each sentence over and over in my head – I could hear Father's voice getting stronger, clearer. After reading the letter for the fourth time, I began to feel oddly connected to him – Henry William Mackenzie – my father, a man I never knew.

But I did know something; I was no longer alone.

*27th April 1851*
*Cable Street*
*Whitechapel*

*Dearest Henry,*

*I have written to you several times since I arrived back in England, but have yet to receive a reply. Maybe you are away at school now, so the letters are being forwarded. I imagine these things take time.*

*You may wonder why I have failed to return home. Or why I have not written to your grandmother. Henry, I cannot. It will be difficult for you to understand. War makes monsters of even the mildest of men. It would distress your grandmother so much to see me like this, and Lord knows she has had enough suffering in her lifetime.*

*Henry, I want you to know that I have thought about you and your dearest mother every day since I left for Afghanistan. How is your mother? To think that it was my lust for adventure that put her in that place! I cannot bear to think on it. Do you go to visit her?*

*I wrote many letters in Afghanistan, but I could not send them. I started to keep a journal, and for a while it helped, and when words failed me I began to draw. Has your grandmother told you that I draw? My journal is not something to look upon lightly, Henry, so be brave; it is the truth of war! The government trade the idea of excitement and glory – they are liars, Henry; I have seen it with my own eyes. It is Hell on earth!*

*I have been very ill since my return and for a long while I could not remember who I was. Fortunately, I had several items of value that I brought back from the East which I could sell to pay my way, but that is all gone now. The landlady's daughter took care of me, making sure I had a sufficiency, but*

*I feel I am long past a recovery so I have sent the girl away. Look out for her, Henry; I believe she is a good girl.*

*I have left a note for the owner of this awful place to make sure my belongings get to you. There's not much left, but… There are also the letters I wrote from Afghanistan, which I could not send for fear of retribution – incompetent officers… Naming names is a dangerous business, Henry. When you read them you'll understand. The whole thing is a damned mess…*

*Always remember, Henry, that I love you dearly, more than you will ever know. If I could change the past I would. Just to be with you, my beloved Emma and your grandmother, but it is too late now. I am so sorry, Henry. I trust one day you will understand.*

*I truly hope and pray that this letter finds you in good health. May God be with you and bless you.*

*With infinite love,*

*Your dearest father*

I sat there for what seemed like ages, thinking about Father's letter. I wasn't sure what I felt. Anger? Frustration? Sadness for the loss of a man I would now never see nor know? Despite myself I began sobbing, and I couldn't stop; it was as if everything that had been bottled up inside of me just had to get out.

I wished I'd spoken to Nana about Father before – before all this. But it had never seemed like the right time. At the beginning, I honestly didn't consider my parents at all, mainly because I'd never known any different. Then, on my tenth birthday, I found a drawing of a woman hidden in Nana's bureau. Nana had sent me to fetch my present, and there it was. I asked Nana about it and she told me it was my mother, but she was no longer with us. I wasn't sure what Nana meant but I had clearly upset her, so I didn't dare ask anything else, and I assumed Mother must have died. Nana had always been so careful about showing her feelings, always disappearing to her room with a headache when it had obviously got too much. So I kept the drawing in my room by my bed – Nana never asked for it back.

I'd asked our housekeeper, Mrs Banks, about Mother, but she'd said it wasn't really her place to say anything. She did tell me stories about how Father had travelled to Florence to study the Great Masters when he was a young man, and how he'd had his drawings exhibited at the Academy. This was how my parents had met, she'd said, through Father's art guild, and they'd fallen in love instantly. Mother had modelled for some of Father's artist friends too. I wished I'd seen the paintings.

I thought about Mrs Banks. I knew she would be out of her mind with worry. And Nana? Nana was the most precious thing in my life – the only connection to my parents – and now she was ill. She'd grown weaker over the last few months and since the discovery at the Great Exhibition and all that followed, Nana had been in bed most days. What if my running away made her worse? What if something happened to the only person who knew the real facts before I had a chance to find out the truth? It didn't bear thinking about.

I folded the letter neatly and placed it inside my jacket pocket. I decided that when Hope awoke I'd insist she show me the way out of this warren, I could find my own way back from Whitechapel. And this time I would ask Nana to tell me where Mother was – if she was still alive. Even if Nana was ill, I wouldn't take no for an answer. All these years I'd believed both my parents were dead, but clearly Father thought Mother was still alive somewhere, and I needed to know where.

Imagine if my mother really was still alive… Maybe there was some hope left…

It was going to be a long night. After having slept half the day it would be near impossible to fall asleep again.

# FLIGHT

# 12

**Henry**

When I woke up, I'd forgotten where I was. I could hear loud voices outside but the words were too faint to make out. And Hope was gone.

Someone was rattling at the windows and doors. I crept over to the small attic window, careful not to make the floorboards creak. I rubbed at the cracked pain of glass with my jacket sleeve; all I could see were hundreds of chimneys belching out thick black clouds of smoke. Outside, the grey damp air clung to the building, seeping in through every crevice. I was freezing. I wondered what time it was; Nana would be worried and more than likely had half the Metropolitan Police Force out looking for me. I hoped they weren't trying to get into the building. Panic rose in me. Where was Hope? My stomach began to rumble and cramp. I thought about the meal I'd refused because of Xavier – especially the lemon pudding. I'd eat anything now.

'Henry! Are you still in there?' Hope whispered from the other side of the wall. 'Give us a hand.' She rattled the side of the cupboard.

I hurried over to the hole in the wall and pushed against the huge piece of furniture that blocked Hope's entrance from the other side with all my strength.

'W-where have you been?' I asked as the cupboard screeched across the floor, wobbling dangerously.

Hope pushed her head through the hole. 'I nipped out to get something to eat. But we have to get out of here – the peelers are outside trying the shop door and windows again. That woman must've insisted they check the shop out.'

'Oh no – do you think they know we're here?' I asked, climbing through the hole into the attic room of the lodging house. The smell of fresh bread and bacon wafted upwards, reminding me of home. 'I'm famished. Did you bring me any food back with you?'

'Is that all you can think about, your belly? And here we are about to be thrown in the clink.'

'Clink?'

'Gaol, Henry! Gaol!' Hope pulled me towards the stairs. 'That's where we'll be going if we get caught! Food can wait till we get away from this place.'

From the top of the stairs I could hear people laughing below. The voices were muffled and sounded far off, but every now and then a screech like a strangled cat rang out over the voices and rolled into hysterical laughing.

'It's the landlady,' said Hope. 'She's cooking the peelers breakfast to keep them sweet.' Hope began to creep down the staircase, keeping tight against the wall. I followed her lead.

'S-sweet?' I said, not knowing what on earth Hope was on about. 'But I thought...'

'Shh!' whispered Hope, putting her finger to her lips. 'So as long as no one comes in, we'll be all right.'

Just as we reached the ground floor, the front door opened. Hope pushed me behind the heavy velvet curtain that hung across the bottom of the stairs.

'Are you looking for the owner of this establishment, sir?' said Hope, approaching the visitor as if she were a resident herself.

'And who are you, may I ask?' said a muffled voice.

I tried to look through a tear in the fabric but a large fern on top of a dresser obscured my view. I thought I recognised the gentleman's voice – it was similar to my uncle's – but it couldn't be, could it?

'I'm a friend, I s'pose you could say,' said Hope. Her speech was affected and high-pitched.

'Don't I know you?' said the gentleman.

'I don't think so, sir. We working girls all look alike,' said Hope, acting much older than she was. 'Can I ask if you're requiring someone particular, sir?'

'Particular? What do you mean?' asked the gentleman, clearly distracted. 'I merely wish to make an enquiry of the two constables I witnessed entering a few moments ago.'

'I see,' murmured Hope, appearing more normal. 'They're all in the parlour, if you want to go through, sir.'

'Thank you… What did you say your name was?'

'I didn't. But you can call me what you fancy…'

The gentleman marched past me towards the back room, his face hidden by his upturned collar. 'I may need to call back this evening; will you be around?'

'Probably, sir,' said Hope after him.

The gentleman laughed. 'I will see you later then.' And with that he knocked hard on the parlour door.

'Quick!' whispered Hope, pulling the curtain back. 'That was your uncle!'

'Xavier?' I peered over the balustrade, but my uncle had disappeared. 'I-I thought the voice sounded familiar. Do you think he's looking for me?'

'I 'spect so,' said Hope. 'But I in't hanging around to find out. Come on.'

We slipped out of the house into the filthy alleyway. 'I think it's best if we find a hideout for a time,' said Hope. 'If your uncle has tipped the wink to the peelers, this place could be crawling any minute.'

The alley was crowded with people sitting around on the cold, damp cobbles or leaning against the walls drunk. Filthy children tugged at their mothers' skirts, crying pitifully. The scene was oppressive, like something straight out of a Dickens book. I wouldn't have believed places like this really existed if I hadn't seen it with my own eyes.

'Come on!' Hope pulled at my jacket. 'I'm in enough trouble already.'

'W-where do you suggest we go?' I said. 'You know I need to get back to Nana. Otherwise, how will I know where my mother is?'

'If she's alive!' said Hope. 'But if your uncle is looking for you, it in't safe for you to go back. Who knows what he's up to?'

'But what about Nana? She'll be w-worried sick,' I said, trying hard not to get angry at Hope.

'You should've thought of that.' Hope grabbed my hand and led me down the numerous miserable alleyways. 'Best we get out of here as soon as possible. Do you have any money?'

'Some,' I said. I didn't really want Hope to know how much, just in case.

'Then call a cab…' said Hope, pushing me into the busy main street. It was a wonder I didn't get run down by the many vehicles rushing up and down the road.

'W-where are we going?'

'I've a friend the other side of the river. He'll know what to do. Tell the driver to take you to Jacob's Island – he'll stop at St Saviour's Dock.'

'W-why don't we use the tunnel?' I asked. 'It'll be far quicker.'

'It's too obvious,' she said. 'And besides, my sort in't allowed.'

As I stepped out onto the road to hail a cab, Hope held back, close to the buildings. 'Aren't you c-coming too?' I said, a sense of panic rising in me.

'It's best we're not seen together,' she said. 'I'll jump on the back; the wheels will hide me.'

Amid all the noise and chaos, I eventually managed to get a cab to stop. I gave him the address Hope had told me and was about to climb on board when the driver said, 'I need to see your money first, if you don't mind, like.' I pulled a half crown from my jacket pocket to prove my solvency, and waved it at him.

'Sorry for asking, only a person can't be too careful nowadays.' He took his hat off and gestured a bow.

'I'm in a hurry,' I said. 'H-how long…?'

'How long, you say? Hard to tell. We'll get there as soon as the old girl puts her mind to it.' He tapped the horse with his whip, and the animal lunged into service. 'Pardon my saying, but you don't look the sorts to be a visiting old Jacob's,' he said before slamming the trapdoor shut.

I hoped I looked like I knew what I was on about, and where I was heading. But in reality, I didn't have a clue. For all I knew, Hope could be leading me to the gates of Hell.

# RUMBLED

# 13

**Hope**

We'd only gone a few yards when the cabby spotted me hanging under his seat. 'Oi, you, get off, you little scrimshanker. I'll get the law on you.' He flicked his whip over his head and caught my arm, forcing me to let go.

I dropped hard onto the busy road, almost getting trampled under the hooves of a following coach and four. I rolled into a ball, praying not to meet my maker. As I got up, I yelled after the cab, 'Stop! Henry!' But Henry mustn't've heard me, 'cause the cab raced on towards London Bridge. I started after it, running as fast as I could, ducking through the traffic and trying to miss the horse muck, which was everywhere. My arm was stinging and a small spot of red started to show through my shawl. *Damn!* I'd never catch up.

I tried to flag down another cab, thinking that Henry could pay when we got there. But no one would stop. It was like I was invisible. I had to get to Jacob's Island before Henry; I daren't think what might happen to him alone. I knew he'd be half terrified, and thinking I'd betrayed him. Somehow I had to make it to Jacob's, and quick. It weren't no place for strangers, and that was for sure.

I ran through the streets, trying hard not to bump into any of Pa's cronies, telling myself I should've hidden better from the driver. Now what?

'Hope!' A voice yelled from across the street.

*Oh, no. That's all I need. Jasper Browne, the biggest mouth in Whitechapel!* Jasper ran across the road, dodging in and out of the traffic like a hound heading the chase.

'Hey, Jasper. What's you doing this far from home?'

'Running an errand, in't I? Got myself a bender if I'm back before the bells.'

'Sixpence! Blimey, who's paying?'

'Some bloated aristocrat. Told me to go check out the bridge to make sure no red-haired toff weren't crossing.'

'Toff! On Jacob's? They'd never get out alive.' I laughed and was about to set off again when Jasper grabbed me by the shoulder.

'Ow, that hurts.' I pushed Jasper away.

'You're bleeding – what you been and done to yourself?'

'Nothing. I slipped, didn't I? It'll be all right.' I rubbed at the cut on my arm, but it just made the bleeding worse.

''Ere,' said Jasper, pulling me to the side of the street. 'Let me see.'

# ALONE

# 14

**Henry**

The cab seemed to charge along at a deadly speed, nothing like Nana's sedate barouche. Drivers raced towards one another, missing a fatal crash by mere seconds. I could hardly bear to look, and at one stage I even covered my eyes for fear of colliding with a huge omnibus. I heard the cabby above shouting obscenities at the unfortunate driver and anyone else who dared cross his path. I thought about poor Hope hanging on for dear life behind me. I should've insisted she rode in the cab.

The stench of the Thames was as thick as the river itself, crawling over everything in its path and settling about my skin and hair, leaving a film of oily slime. Instinctively, I rubbed at my face with my jacket sleeve, but it only seemed to exaggerate the claustrophobic feeling of disgust that enveloped me. I wondered how long it would be until we reached Jacob's Island. I tapped on the roof and the driver opened the trapdoor.

'How much longer?' I asked.

'Not long, mister. Would've been a might faster if that delinquent 'adn't been 'angin' off me seat.'

'What do you mean?'

'Some slip of a girl trying to filch a free ride. But I soon sorted 'er out, don't you worry.'

*Oh no, Hope.*

'Stop the coach!'

# A Near Miss

# 15

**Hope**

It seemed Jasper fancied himself as a physician or something, coming over all concerned. Taking his kerchief from his grimy neck, he tied it around my arm. 'That should do it,' he said, pulling the knot tighter. 'Anyways, where's you off to in such a hurry?'

'Nowhere that's any of your business,' I said, fiddling with his makeshift bandage and trying to sound bored. I didn't want to raise his curiosity. It weren't that Jasper was *all* bad; he was all right in his own ways. He just didn't know how to keep a secret. But worse than that, somehow he always managed to get it out of a person. And then blab to everyone.

'Sounds like you hiding something to me. I'll give you a penny if you tell.'

'I in't hiding nothing. Besides, in't you supposed to be somewhere?'

The clock of the old church started to strike.

One.

Two.

Three...

'Nah. You walking back to Whitechapel?' said Jasper, snatching some bread off a passing cart. 'We could walk together if you like.'

'I thought you were watching the bridge?'

Four.

Five.

Six…

'Watched it already. No toff I saw with red hair. But if you're going that ways I could check again…'

Ten!

Henry would be there by now. God only knows what would happen to him.

'Well?' Jasper wasn't going to give up easy. 'You walking back or what?'

'I…I in't sure. I…'

'Oh, for Christ's sake, Hope. Are you or in't you?'

'No,' I said. 'It's my aunt what lives over the water. She's not feeling good. Ma said I've to go look after the little-uns – she might've caught the sickness.'

'Rather you than me. I can't stand flipping screaming brats – got plenty at home meself! Might catch you later then?'

Just as Jasper turned to leave, I heard Henry, shouting at the top of his voice. 'Hope! Hope! Over here…'

Oh no.

Jasper looked at me, then at Henry, who was half hanging out of the hansom cab, waving his cap, his bright red hair catching the wretched morning sun.

'The toff!' said Jasper.

'Jasper, please—'

'I thought you said…'

I charged towards the oncoming cab with Jasper inches behind, grabbing at my shawl, then my skirts. Just as Jasper gained a hold on me, Henry leapt from the moving cab and thumped Jasper hard in the eye. *Bam!* Just like that. Jasper slipped and fell face down into horse muck, rubbish and straw.

Taking my hand, Henry started back towards the cab. 'Are you hurt?' he said, looking at Jasper's dirty yellow-spotted kerchief.

'I'll be all right.'

The cabby pulled the horse to a stop. 'What's going on? You all right, mister?'

'Fine. Thank you.' Henry opened the door and helped me up into the cab, then hopped in next to me.

'I in't never been in no cab before,' I said, as Henry pulled the door shut.

'Then I hope you like it,' said Henry, smiling for the first time since we'd met.

Henry tapped the roof and shouted up to the driver. 'Jacob's Island!' The driver cracked his whip and we lurched forward. As the cab turned around I heard Jasper cursing and screaming after us.

'Hope! That sixpence is as good as mine. You'll see…'

'Who was that?' asked Henry.

'A blabbermouth and a two-face who has his eye on making himself some money,' I said.

# HANSOM CAB

# 16

**Henry**

'You need to get that cut looked at – we s-should go back,' I said to Hope. The neckerchief the boy had wrapped around it was filthy, more likely to make her wound worse than better.

'We can't go back. Jasper said your uncle sent looking for you.'

'Then we'll stop at an alehouse and get some wine.'

'Wine? What for?'

'I read somewhere that the Ancient Greeks bathed w-wounds in wine to help prevent infection,' I said. 'And the sooner the better.'

'Driver?' I shouted up through the trapdoor. 'W-where is the nearest tavern?'

'The Old Brown Bear, just ahead. You want me to stop?'

'Yes. And w-wait for me.'

A minute or two later, the cab stopped. 'Here you are. Watch yourself in there.'

I was about to get down from the cab when Hope held me back. 'You can't go. You might be spotted. I'll go.'

I gave Hope a shilling and waited. Outside the tavern an argument seemed to be getting out of control. A woman with a child tied on her back was fighting with a girl not much older than Hope, who was hanging onto a man's arm.

'Here I am with five mouths to feed,' said the woman. 'And you're drinking and wasting our last pennies on tarts.'

''Ere, who you calling a tart, you old hag? In't no wonder he drinks!' The girl grabbed hold of the woman's hair and started pulling her to the ground. The baby was crying, clearly distressed. The crowd was closing in – pushing, whooping and hollering – making the horse skittish.

'Excuse me, mister,' said the driver. 'We should go. This could turn ugly.'

'W-wait,' I said. 'W-we need to wait for Hope. I mean, the young lady.'

'Not sure if I can…'

Then Hope's face appeared at the side of the cab. 'Oi, let me up.'

I opened the doors and pulled her into the cab. 'Did you get some wine?'

'And more besides!' she said, grinning.

The cab jolted forward as the horse was whipped into service again. Above the screaming, shouting, hysterical crowd, I heard the ratchet of a constable's rattle several times.

Hope held up a stout greenish bottle. 'Wine!' she said, pulling out the stopper with her teeth and taking a sip. 'Yuk! That's disgusting!' After handing me the bottle she produced half a pork pie and two eggs from her skirt pockets. 'And breakfast!'

'Did you have enough money?' I asked, taking the bottle and food from her.

'And got some change an' all,' she said, handing me two silver three-penny coins.

As the hansom cab settled into an even pace I removed the rag from Hope's arm. The cut was long, but fortunately not too deep. I poured the wine over the wound and the dark liquid ran down Hope's arm and onto her ripped shawl. Taking my silk handkerchief, I tied it around Hope's wound. 'That should feel better,' I said. 'Now it's clean and dressed.'

'Thanks,' said Hope, pulling the shawl back around her shoulders. 'Are you hungry?'

'St-st-starving,' I said, breaking the pork pie in two. 'I feel like I haven't eaten for days.' My appetite was enormous, probably from all the excitement!

As the cab rattled towards London Bridge, the dark skeletal shapes of the sail-less prison ships creaked and groaned as they tried hard to hold onto their criminal cargo. What kind of place was I going to?

We sat in silence for what felt like ages. I wondered why Hope was risking so much for me. After I'd finished eating and was about to take a sip of wine, I realised Hope hadn't touched her food. She was just sitting there, staring ahead blankly.

'Is something wrong?' I asked. 'Do you feel f-faint or something?'

'It's Jasper,' she said.

'J-Jasper? The boy, back there? You're not w-worried about him, are you?'

'No. Yes. I… If he tells your uncle we're together…' she broke off. 'It's Ma. I don't think she can take another beating.'

'W-what do you mean? Xavier will beat her?'

'No. But he might as well. Once word gets out we're together, Pa will make her talk.'

'T-talk? Talk about what? She doesn't know w-where we're going, does she?'

'It won't take her long to work it out. I always run back to Jacob's.'

'W-why on earth are we going there then?'

'A friend. A close friend. He'll know how to get hold of your pa's letters. That's what you want, in't it? So we can find out if your ma is alive and, if she is, where they've put her.'

This was the first time Hope had mentioned the other letters. She'd said she'd help me find my mother, but I hadn't thought to ask how.

'The letters your ma mentioned?'

'Yeah. I in't sure, but I think Pa took them and gave them to your uncle. I think they're going to blackmail your nana.'

'What did the letters say?'

'How do I know? I in't seen them, have I?' Hope rubbed at her arm. 'Usually it's secrets – things people don't want known, or are ashamed of...'

'Usually? Has your family done this before?' I was frightened of Hope's world, but I wasn't going to stop now. Hope didn't reply.

'H-how will this friend get the letters?' I asked, feeling really frustrated with myself for not having thought through how Hope could help me. 'I guess he'll want money too?'

'I don't know, maybe. Henry...?'

'Yeah?'

'Your father gave me this... He said you'd know it was from him.' Hope handed me a pocket watch and I recognised our family crest immediately.

'W-why has it taken you so long to...'

'Don't ask me, Henry. Security, I guess.'

It must've taken a lot for Hope to give me the watch – it was of considerable value, and could have fed her family for months. I appreciated Hope's honesty. 'Thank you; it means a great deal to me.'

Moments later, the cab came to a sudden stop and the trap-door in the roof opened. 'St Saviour's Dock. This is as far as I go.'

I reached through the trapdoor and paid the driver a good tip on top of his fee. 'If anyone asks about m-me, or this young l-lady, you haven't seen us, understood?'

The driver nodded. 'Course not – your secret's safe with me.'

Hope looked at me as she jumped down from the cab. 'Young lady, eh? Never been called that before in all my born days.'

'So, where do we go now?' I said, slipping the watch and the bottle of wine in my pocket.

# DEN OF THIEVES

# 17

**Henry**

Hope grabbed hold of my jacket and started to pull at the sleeve. 'W-what are you doing?' I said, not sure if I was about to be mugged.

'Got to get rid of your clothes; you'll be spotted a mile off. Take off your coat and waistcoat, and roll up your sleeves.'

I did as I was told. Then Hope bent down and dipped her hands in the filthy mud that enveloped the road.

'W-what are you...?'

Before I could object, Hope wiped her mucky hands across my face and down my arms. 'This'll make you blend in,' she said.

'Thanks!'

So this was Jacob's Island? Even at this early hour, the place was crowded. The ships on the river were like a vast city, the huge masts jutting up into the sky making me think of the woodland that surrounded our Scottish home – where stayed throughout the summer months when it was unbearably hot in London. I couldn't imagine living in this place, so close to the stinking Thames, all year.

'Oi, we in't got all day,' Hope said, marching on ahead. 'If we want to find out about your ma, we need to get those letters.'

'W-where're we going?'

'A friend's. I told you already.'

'But you didn't say who,' I protested. 'W-who is this friend?'

'You'll find out soon enough.'

We made our way across the rotting wooden bridges, towards the buildings that looked like they were built on a quagmire, swathes of thick slime below us. I thought about Dickens' character, Bill Sikes, who'd accidently hanged himself while trying to escape justice – now I could see why. Ropes hung from every rooftop, window and footbridge, like the kraken's tendrils, trailing into the filthy river below – waiting for some fool to stumble by. The wooden planks that made up the bridges were rotted through in places. Even the posts that held everything above the waterline leant at awkward angles.

Within five minutes we'd reached our destination. The building looked derelict. Hope banged on the door and walked straight in. 'George! Tosher! Crooner! It's me, Hope.' Moments later the trio appeared through a hatch in the floor.

'Thought you were the bleedin' law, didn't we?' The short, round lad shoved Hope in the shoulder, nearly knocking her over. His two near identical friends were at least a foot taller, but half his width.

'We need your help,' said Hope, straightening herself up. 'This is Henry, and he's Mac's boy, so I don't want no funny business, right?'

'Course not,' said the round one. 'Wouldn't dream of it, would we, lads?'

'No, course not, George,' echoed the other two.

I put my hand out to shake theirs, but Hope stepped in front of me. 'We in't got time to play friendly gents. Come on.' We all followed Hope up two flights of stairs and along a terrace, which ran the length of the building. In through another door, we went down another flight of stairs, which was falling apart. It was a true rabbit's warren, to say the least.

'W-where are w-we going?' My nerves were getting the better of me; I tried breathing deeply but the sulphurous atmosphere nearly made me choke.

'W-w-w-where… W-w-where are we g-going?' One of the boys mimicked me, and they all started laughing. I could feel myself getting hot around my neck, and I turned to face the boys behind me. I shoved George in the chest and he stumbled back, knocking into the other two. I'd caught him off guard.

'Oi, we was only having a bit of fun, weren't we, Tosher?' George elbowed the first of the other boys. I noticed he had a red, raw-looking patch on his lower jawline, which his twin didn't. Now I knew who was who.

'Stop messing about!' said Hope, as she squeezed through a hole in the wall.

The sound of corroded metal against metal and banging on the opposite side of the wall soon revealed a secret opening into a room that overlooked the whole entrance to the dock – a great lookout post.

'We'll be safe here,' Hope said. 'This'll be our headquarters. All reporting back comes to me. Make sure you're not followed. If you think someone's on your tail, you duck and dive and lead them back to the beginning. You never come back here. Got it?'

'Yeah, all right, captain,' George touched his brow, which made the twins snigger.

'This in't a game,' said Hope. 'It's a matter of life and death. That's why we've come to you, George, 'cause you're the best.'

George suddenly became all serious. 'You listening, Tosher? Crooner?'

'Yes, George.'

The room was dark except for the shaft of light coming through the hole where a window had been boarded up. There were a few large packing cases, and a table with a stool underneath. On the floor, layers of newspaper covered the main area, like one of Nana's Axminster Rugs.

'George! You got any grub?' asked Hope. 'We've not got enough for everyone.'

'We've got a hock of cooked ham we nicked from…'

'Tosher! What did I tell you? Never tell no one about having no food!' George clipped his friend around the ear, which must've hurt because Tosher held his hand over it for some time.

'Right,' said Hope. 'We need to make a pact. While we're in this together, we share everything, right?' She put her hand out in front of her and the boys formed a circle around her, each placing their hands on top of the other. I waited for the ritual to end but they all stood still, looking at me. 'Well?' said Hope. 'Are you in or not? After all, it's your neck on the line if we fail.'

I shuffled closer to Hope and placed my hand on top of Tosher's. 'I w-want to say,' I said, 'that I really appreciate w-what you're all—'

'Yeah, yeah,' George interrupted. 'Let's get on with it.'

Hope took the lead. 'We all swear, on our lives, that we tell no lies to each other while we're helping Henry. That we share our food. And we watch each other's backs – even at the cost of our own.' The little group looked at each other with such intensity I feared that, if I were the enemy, they could finish me off with one glance.

'I swear,' said George.

'Swear,' echoed Tosher and Crooner together.

'Swear,' said Hope.

'I s-s-swear,' I said.

80

'Now seal it,' said George, before we withdrew our hands. Pulling his hand from the pile, he spat hard into the middle of his palm. 'To the death!' he said, dramatically. And the entire group spat on their palms and slapped it into George's, one by one. Although I felt disgusted, I did the same. For the first time in my life, I felt as though I was part of something.

Crooner went off to get the ham and Hope pulled cheese, bread and cooked sausage from her bag. I still had the wine in my jacket pocket, which I put with the food. George immediately grabbed hold of the bottle and smashed it on the floor.

'Eh, w-what are you doing? That was all we had to drink,' I said. George stormed off, and Tosher chased after him.

'Leave it, Henry,' said Hope, dividing the food up. 'It's George's ma, that's all.'

'W-what about her?' I whispered.

'George's pa beat his ma when he was drunk one time. It was the first time he'd drunk wine; some say it must've been a bad bottle. Anyway, his ma died later and his pa was... Well, George don't like having no drink about.'

'Oh, I see,' I said. 'So w-where does George live now? If his parents are...well...?'

Hope finished sharing the food and wiped her hands down her skirt. 'Same as the rest of the gang,' she said. 'Here and there. You don't ask no questions round here. Could find yourself at the bottom of Old Father Thames.'

The boys returned with the ham and some cress, which Tosher said he'd found earlier. It wasn't the best meal I'd ever eaten, but it tasted like a feast.

# MAKING PLANS

# 18

**Hope**

'First we've to find out where the letters are,' I said, after we'd all finished eating. 'Chances are they'll be with Henry's uncle; I'm sure he's mixed up in this.'

'W-what makes you think Xavier's involved?' asked Henry. 'Just because he came to Whitechapel doesn't mean he's implicated.'

'Impl... what?' said Tosher. 'Speak proper English, will you!'

'It just means mixed up in it, Tosher,' said George. 'He's just showing off. In't you?'

'No. I—'

'We don't know, Henry, not for sure. But his being in Whitechapel and knowing my ma an' all... Well, it makes for suspicion, wouldn't you say?' I didn't mention that Xavier was a regular at Ma's house neither.

The boys started pushing each other around, just like they always did when they were bored. Crooner fell and hit his head. 'Ow!'

'Stop arguing! We've got to work out a plan,' I said. 'Right, Henry, do you know where your uncle lives?'

'He's got a house in Cheltenham. But when he's in London he stays at one of his clubs. The Oriental, I think.'

'George, do you know anyone at that club? Someone you can *really* trust?'

'There might be someone, but...' George got up and paced the room. 'Trouble is, they're all paid well to keep secrets,' he said before sitting back down again. 'And I in't sure I can persuade no one to snitch on their guvnor, like.'

'W-would money h-help?' Henry asked, taking out his purse. 'If we paid them, maybe they'd feel inclined?'

'There he goes again, speaking all posh so as to swindle us,' said Tosher. 'It makes me right mad, so it does.'

'I'm not trying to s-swindle anyone,' said Henry. 'Quite the opposite.'

'For crying out loud! Can everyone stop yapping for two minutes?' I'd begun to think I'd made a mistake coming to George and his boys, but they were the best in London for quick results. No sooner than a cove could say 'Jack Robinson', the boys would get answers.

Over the past year I'd spoken to George about Mac, and George had kept it secret from everyone, just like I'd asked. So I knew I could trust him with my life. When Mac died, I came straight to Jacob's to ask George for help – that was when he told Crooner and Tosher, 'cause by then they had to know, he said.

'W-what's the plan then, Hope?' Henry was up now and circling the room. He still had his jacket and waistcoat tucked under his arm, like he was afraid they'd disappear if he put them down, and he'd be right.

'I in't sure. If we go anywhere near your uncle's, we're bound to get spotted, 'specially you...'

'Yeah, with that carrot top!' said Tosher, shoving Crooner in the ribs. Tosher had a point – Henry's hair was long and wavy, and the red russet colour would be easily spied.

'We'll have to cut it off,' I said. 'You got a knife, George?'

'Course I 'ave.' He pulled a piece of metal shaped to a point from his belt. ''Ere,' he said, handing me his blade.

'Blimey, George, what am I s'posed to do with this?' The knife was sharp at the point, but the sides were rusty and jagged. 'If I use this, his head'll be redder than his bleeding hair!'

The boys laughed and started larking about again. Then Henry took something out of his jacket pocket.

'I have a knife.' He handed me the leather and metal encased knife. As I pulled it from its sheath, the blade caught the sunlight that streamed through a chink in the wood, and the room danced with little scraps of light.

'Cor, look at that why don't you.' Crooner was suddenly beside me, staring at the knife like it was the crown jewels or something. 'Where did you get it, Henry?'

'It's my father's,' said Henry. 'I mean, *w-was* my father's – it was in his belongings. From Hope's h-home…'

'It must be worth a fortune,' said George, stroking the blade. 'How come your pa didn't filch the knife, Hope?'

'Dunno. Must be worth a bob or two.'

'It must be our family crest,' said Henry. 'It's on everything. It would be too easy to identify – if someone tried to s-sell it, I mean. A buyer might be a bit wary.' Henry obviously didn't know my world.

Henry sat down on one of the boxes and, taking his cap off, he said, 'Get on with it then, before I change my mind.'

The blade was sharp and I nearly cut myself several times. Henry's hair was thick and it took a lot of hacking, but in the end I made a fairly good job of it. When he put his cap back on there wasn't a strand of copper hair to be seen.

'Now you're one of us,' said Tosher, which made Henry laugh.

**84**

'So what, when and where?' said George. 'I 'ate waiting – that's when things go all wrong.'

'Someone's got to get inside the club, search Henry's uncle's personals and, if the letters are there, take them. If not, see if there's any clue as to where they might be.' It sounded straightforward enough, but first we'd to get past the porter, and that would be tricky.

George suddenly piped up, 'I do know someone. But…'

'But what?' I asked.

'It's the housekeeper's daughter,' said George, heading for the secret door. 'I think she's a little sweet on me. But I don't want her getting no ideas, like.' George stopped and smiled. 'But just for you, Hope, I'll find out when this Xavier gent is out and get her to leave his room door unlocked.'

'Thanks, George,' I said.

'Come on, you two,' said George to Tosher and Crooner. 'We've work to do.' And all three of them vanished.

'W-what shall we do?' Henry asked, keen to follow the others. 'If the boys get the letters, we could go straight to the Courts of Justice and foil Xavier's plans.'

'Hang on, Henry. Firstly, they're only going to look. And we don't know for certain that your uncle's part of the con yet.' Although I was pretty convinced, I didn't want to point the finger at Henry's family. Not until we had *real* proof.

'Second, even if Xavier is involved, we don't know who else might be part of it. Does your uncle know any lawyers or judges that might use the club? Third, you don't want to be too hasty – we need to get the letters and see what they say. Your nana might not want everyone knowing the family business, like.'

Henry scratched at his scalp. 'I guess you're right; I just can't bear w-waiting.'

'Who said we're waiting? I thought we could go swap some of your lovely togs for some useful ones. Mr Arnold the ragman will give us a good deal.'

'R-ragman? This is a brand new mourning suit; it cost my nana a f-fortune! She'd kill me – or, at least, Mrs Banks would.'

'Do you want to get caught? In that getup you'll stand out a mile. If we sell your suit, we'll have enough brass to buy food for everyone, *and* get you some clobber.'

# DISGUISE

# 19

**Henry**

The journey through Jacob's Island was really unpleasant. The river stank of rotten eggs and if you dared look over the edge of the rickety footbridges you could see the sulphuric acid bubbling to the top like a volcano waiting to erupt. The *Morning Chronicle* called it the Venice of drains – I could see why. To think, thousands of people lived here in this open sewer and Hope knew practically all of them. I felt she was putting us at risk, being seen together, so I tried to make myself as inconspicuous as possible.

'That your beau, Hope?' shouted an old lady hanging out her washing. 'Looks like you've bagged a rich one there…'

Hope just laughed and ignored the woman.

'See,' I said. 'People know I'm not from round here. They could fetch the police and we'd be caught in no time.'

'Tell the peelers? Folk round here has better things to do with their time than stick their noses into your business. Christ, Henry, are you blind?'

'W-what do you mean?' I felt insulted. Of course I could see life was difficult and I said so.

'Difficult? Difficult you say? How's about you trying to feed your kids when your old man's drunk all his wages? That's if he even has a job. Or…or pay the rent when the fat landlord comes calling.'

Hope's face hardened and I hated myself for not being more sensitive. It was the first time I'd seen Hope angry and the way her mouth tightened and the skin across her cheekbones seemed to protrude told me not to dwell on the subject. For the next ten minutes, we didn't speak; Hope stormed on ahead and I had to run to keep up. It was hard work trying to hang onto my jacket and stop myself slipping on the green slime that covered every surface.

'Come on. We're nearly there,' called Hope, sounding a lot calmer. She stopped to wait for me to catch up. 'Here, we'd better brush your clothes down to make sure we get the best price.'

'W-what will the tailor think – me exchanging my suit for…' I paused, not wanting to upset Hope again. 'Um, for…some other clothes.'

'Tailor! Henry, you do make me laugh.' Hope punched my arm and smiled. I figured the punch was a gesture of endearment. But it was lovely to see Hope's face brighten up.

'Now, if Mr Arnold asks any questions, make out you're a mute – leave me to do the talking.' Hope was serious again.

When we opened the door of the Trading Post, it was like walking into Aladdin's cave, but instead of jewels and gold, the shop was hung with silk handkerchiefs, waistcoats of every colour, dress coats, top hats, pantaloons and ladies' frocks in purple, blue, mustard and crimson. I couldn't believe it – a place like this, in the quagmire of Jacob's. Even the rotting fish and eggs that permeated every inch of Jacob's Island was absent in this little haven – I wanted to stay and breathe in the smell of coffee and eucalyptus.

At first I thought the shop was empty, and then a small bald man, with tiny wire-framed spectacles, appeared around the side of the counter – which was piled high with clothes.

'What's you two want? Selling your grandma's silver?'

The man, who I assumed was Mr Arnold, chuckled at his own quip. As he got close enough to see us through his glasses, he stopped and eyed me up and down.

'Well, this is an interesting specimen, if I say so myself. In't from around here, are you?'

'Uh, no,' I said, before Hope elbowed me in the side. 'I mean yes…' I didn't see the point in lying – it was obvious to everyone that I was an outsider – but Hope knew what she was doing.

'I don't want no questions, Mr Arnold, but we have 'ere a nice example of a gentleman's suit.' Hope stood back and swept her hands up and down in front of me as if I were a circus freak. 'Show him the jacket, Henry.' I held it up. 'And we'd like to exchange it for some of our dear Queen's brass.'

'Would you now?' said Mr Arnold, moving closer.

Taking my jacket from me, he turned it inside out, and back again. Holding the fabric to his nose, he sniffed at it like a dog. 'Interesting. Harris Tweed! Shorn and woven on one of the islands.'

I looked at Hope, and she looked at me and shrugged. This man was definitely a little odd – was he playing with us?

'Lewis!' he exclaimed. 'Definitely Lewis.'

He handed me back my jacket and I immediately felt the pockets to make sure he hadn't emptied them in his stage performance. My father's letter, knife and watch were still there, thank goodness. I was a fool to have left my valuables in the jacket. Fortunately, I'd given Hope my father's sketchbook earlier.

'Well?' said Hope. 'What do you think?'

'I think this young man means trouble,' he said. 'Expensive trouble. Not interested.'

'W-what do you mean?' I said. 'These clothes belong to me and if I choose to sell them, then I shall.' Hope scowled at me.

'Shall you indeed?' said Mr Arnold, sitting down in an old armchair. 'In case you hadn't realised, young man, in order to sell an item, you needs to have a buyer what's prepared to buy. And I in't!'

'But w-why?' I asked. 'I don't understand…'

'An h-educated person such as yourself not understand? Well, that's a first.'

Mr Arnold began lecturing me about ''aving all the h-opportunities of an h-education, but still being stupid'. Hope kept quiet and wandered around the small shop, touching the items that littered every surface, shelf and hook.

'Oi, don't try to trick me, madam, with your distractions. Get back here and stop dirtyin' me stock!'

'Mr Arnold?' said Hope. 'I notice you've a fine lady's purse for sale; I was wondering, like, where you got it from.' Hope held up a rich, green velvet purse, decorated in fine jewels.

'That's none of your business!' said Mr Arnold, leaping from his chair and snatching the purse from Hope's hand. 'Look, you've dirtied the velvet!' he said, taking a small brush from his pocket and gently dusting the purse.

'Only, I've reason to believe…' said Hope. 'That there purse looks suspiciously like the one what was reported as stolen. Belonged to the Chief Commissioner's wife, so I 'eard – I'm sure he'd be interested in its whereabouts.'

I looked at Hope – how did she know where the purse came from? Was she bluffing? Hope stood her ground and waited for Mr Arnold to say something. A minute or two later he obliged.

'All right, all right, you win. But if it brings trouble to my door, I'll be pointing my finger in your direction. Understand?'

So the deal was done. My boots, tweed mourning suit, waistcoat, cap and linen shirt were sold for some filthy, ragged counterparts and five shillings and six pence.

# NEWS

# 20

**Hope**

'If I didn't know better, Henry Mackenzie, I'd say you were a local…'

'Thanks for the compliment, I think…' Henry was dragging behind, and scratching at his arms and legs as if he'd fleas.

'It's best we get back to the hiding place, as soon as possible. George and the boys will be back and ready to act,' I said, making sure the flap of my satchel was buckled tight. Henry had given me his pa's things at Mr Arnolds, to keep safe, as all his pockets now had holes in them. I was worried that if I slipped near the river, the whole lot would be lost, including the watch and the only letter Henry had from his pa.

'Hope? Do you think there's a chance my mother is still alive?' Henry's voice was so quiet; I could barely hear him over the noise on Jacob's. I stopped and waited for him to catch up.

'Dunno. Mac, I mean, your pa, thought so. Why would he say what he said in the letter, if it's not true? I mean…'

'It's just Father has been gone for years. I don't ever remember him being around. M-mother neither. And surely, *if* she is alive, Nana or Mrs Banks would've said something?'

'I'm not sure,' I said, squeezing Henry's shoulder. 'Thing is, people don't always tell the truth, and sometimes it can be for the best reasons.'

I thought about Ma and how nasty she could be to me, but I knew, underneath it all, she was just trying to protect me in her own way.

'Come on, let's get back,' I said, shoving Henry in front of me. 'It'll be all right in the end, as my ma says.'

When we returned to the room, George and the boys were waiting.

'Well, that Xavier geezer *is* staying at The Oriental...' said George.

'And...' added Tosher. 'Guess what?'

'W-what?' said Henry.

'He's only going home to the country for a few days,' chimed in Crooner. 'Elsie, the girl who fancies George, looks after his room, and is packing his trunk as we speak.'

'So we've got to make a move now,' said George. 'Or it'll be too late.'

'H-how? W-won't Uncle Xavier be at the club now, if he's about to leave?' Henry started pacing the room. 'W-what do you think, Hope?'

The bell at the sailor's mission rang out...

*Bong.*

*Bong.*

*Bong.*

'Perfect timing,' I said. 'It's lunchtime. If we hurry, Xavier might be at the Olde Cheshire Cheese, supping. Everyone goes there. And the coach in't leaving until seven.'

As the bell struck twelve, George said, 'Great, we can get in his room whilst he's stuffing his face.'

'Come on then,' said Henry. 'How long will it take to get there, George?'

'As long as it takes. And longer if you hang about yacking.'

As we made our way towards the bridge, everyone was talking at once, except Henry who seemed to be miles away in another world.

'You all right?' I asked, slowing down. 'Only you don't look too happy. Sure you want to do this?'

'I've got to. It's my only chance to find out the truth. If Xavier's involved he's bound to have the letters. If not…'

'If not, what?'

'If not. Then I don't know. I guess s-somehow we'll have to get your p-pa to talk.'

'My pa! But…I can't go back there, Henry.' I could feel my face and neck begin to tighten; I shook myself to try to relieve the stress. 'Pa has plans.'

'Plans?'

'Yeah.' I didn't want to think about it – but sooner or later I'd have to face Pa. 'If I go back now… Pa says I'm *special*, don't you know!'

'Special? I don't understand?'

'Course you don't, Henry. Why would you?'

The boys were hanging back, listening to what I was saying. They knew only too well what the sale would mean. 'I can't go back, Henry, Pa will… If I don't… He'll kill me if I go home.' Even Henry could understand that surely… 'I'm sorry, Henry, I can't, not even for you.'

When we got near to the club, George said he'd have a look around, just in case Xavier was still about. But Henry wanted to make sure George didn't miss nothing, and kept insisting on going with him.

'Don't you trust me?' said George, looking like he was ready to fight Henry.

'It's not that,' said Henry. 'It's just…I need to be sure…'

'I can be sure. As much as you can anyhow!'

'For God's sake,' I said. 'Just let Henry go with you.'

'But what if he's spotted,' said Tosher. 'I'm not going down for no toff.'

I turned to Henry who was scuffing his shoes into the dirt. 'Listen, George has a point. If anything goes wrong, we'll all be for the clink. Old Judge Jeffreys is as mean as they get.'

It took a while to get Henry to agree, as he still wanted to be close enough to see what was happening. In the end he gave in, but insisted that I went with George, while he and the twins kept watch.

As me and George slipped past the porter, George's girl hurried out of the building. 'Mr Xavier's in his room,' Elsie said. 'He said he weren't eating till later as he'd business to see to.' The girl looked terrified and I didn't blame her – if she got caught, not only would she be out of a job, she might even be put before the Beak. 'You've got to go! If you get seen… I don't know what—' she cut herself off, clearly not wanting to think about what might happen. 'He says he's having supper with an old friend before he catches the evening carriage.'

'Right, Elsie, we best come back later then,' said George. 'We'll meet here when the prison ships sound the rest horn.'

I gave the boys sixpence of Henry's money to get some grub, and the promise of sixpence more to make sure they'd come back when they said they would – they'd do anything for food. The boys raced off and were gone within a blink of an eye.

'W-who said you could hand out *my* money?' Henry was annoyed, I could tell; I was beginning to recognise the signs.

'It's *our* money, Henry. Until this is over, everything is shared. Remember?'

'Oh, yeah.'

I looked at Henry – his disguise was really convincing, but it was pitiful to see him looking so ragged. Henry could easily pass for one of us, until he spoke; then he couldn't help but give the game away.

'Listen, we best not hang around here,' I said. 'I know a place nearby where we won't be bothered.'

As we walked along Regent Street, Henry looked as if he might faint from starvation at any moment. I was hungry myself, but I was used to surviving on a hunk of bread and cheese. Henry would probably guzzle at one meal as much as I'd have in a week.

I knew an old churchyard near the Olde Cheshire Cheese. It was deserted when we got there, except for an old man who looked to be putting flowers on a grave.

'I've always liked walking around here and imagining what people's lives were like. Now they're all dead and forgotten,' I said, before remembering Henry's pa and all. 'Sorry, Henry, I didn't...'

Henry didn't answer; he was busy looking at the headstones, and rubbing the dirt and growth off so he could read them.

'I wonder if my father is buried here?' Henry went from one tombstone to another, like a spectre searching for its home.

'Course he in't,' I said. 'He's barely cold in the ground...' I shut up quickly as I could see Henry was upset. 'Even if he is, he won't have no headstone, will he? No one knew who he was... And anyways, this place is for the rich...'

Henry looked at me in disbelief. 'But Father is rich – I mean; he was...'

As we walked around the back of the church, there was a huge tomb with an angel on top. I'd never noticed it before. At the angel's feet there was a small bunch of pale blue forget-me-nots, starting to wilt.

'Hey, look at this Henry.'

Henry joined me at the foot of the angel. 'When I die, Henry, will you put an angel on my grave? Only I don't want to be dumped in no mass pauper's grave.' Huge yew trees surrounded the tomb, and birds' muck had dripped down the angel's face, streaking the red marble with white. It looked as if the angel had been crying. I thought about Mac dying alone. 'I don't want to die alone, Henry. I hate being on my own.'

'W-we're all alone,' said Henry, spitting on his sleeve and wiping the writing at the foot of the tomb. 'In the end we're always alone.'

'Don't sound so cheerful,' I said, annoyed that I'd even mentioned it. 'Come on, let's find somewhere to sit down – I'm done in.'

'H-hang on.' Henry started rubbing like a mad man at the wording on the tombstone. 'Look! It says "Mackenzie" – it could be Father…'

'Henry, I just said…'

'Look, Hope.' Henry pointed at the carved out lettering, and started to read aloud: '"William Henry Mackenzie. In the hands of our Lord. Born 1770, died 1842." It must be my grandfather.' Henry brushed wildly at the fallen leaves. 'Why hasn't Nana brought me here? My father should be buried here; it's the family grave.'

I sat on a stump nearby and watched as Henry tried to clean the tomb with a scrap of newspaper that had been blowing around the graves. After a while Henry knelt down and started talking to himself. I couldn't make out the words – he was muttering in a language I didn't know.

'What you saying?' I got up and shoved Henry. 'Talk English! No secrets! You promised.'

Henry looked up at me like I was an idiot. 'It's Latin… Don't you know your scripture?'

'Sounds like Devil worship to me…'

# CONFESSIONS

# 21

## Hope

We wandered around the back of the church and found a large willow tree overhanging a wall. It was leaning so far into the churchyard some of its branches almost touched the floor, making a shaded den to hide in.

I pushed the large branches out of the way to create an opening.

'Perfect,' I said. 'No one will see us here.' I held the half-broken branch up so Henry could crawl in and added, 'We can sleep for a couple of hours; it might be a long day.'

The ground was quite dry under the tree; dead leaves, dried grass and mud made a natural carpet. Henry sat down and leant against the wall. For a while he sat with his arms wrapped around his shins and his forehead resting on top of his knees. I didn't speak as Henry seemed to be trying to sleep – he was rocking himself back and forth as though the rhythm would help. After a while, his head fell back against the wall and his eyes were closed. The silence was deafening; I could hear the hum of my blood pulsating in my ears. After a while I couldn't stand the total quietness any longer.

'You asleep, Henry?'

'No.' Henry opened his eyes. 'I was trying to though.'

'Sorry. It's just the silence...'

'I know...'

'I don't mind the quiet sometimes,' I said. 'It gives me time to think.'

'I hate it.'

'Why?'

Henry picked up a stick and started drawing in the dry mud. 'I guess it's just so quiet at home,' he said. 'Before Nana's illness, it was bearable.' In the dusty dirt floor, a face began to take shape. 'Most nights after dinner we'd play games, or Nana would read to Mrs Banks and me, mainly Mr Dickens, our favourite.' Henry smiled. 'And during the day I had Mr Jameson, my tutor...'

The face in the dirt looked similar to the one that was in the *Illustrated London News* – the newspaper I'd been forced to deliver to Henry. 'Is that your ma?' I said, pointing at the picture.

Henry scooted his foot across the floor, erasing the image. 'I can't draw. Not like my father, anyhow.'

'It was good. You should keep practising.'

'Maybe.'

For a while we sat and chatted about nothing. Henry asked me about my ma and pa, and I told him that my real pa was dead, and Albert – Ma's man – had moved in to 'look after us'. Only it hadn't turned out like that. I tried to change the subject but Henry carried on.

'W-what do you mean? I know it must be hard, but at least you have a house, and food. Some people...'

'Yeah, I'm grateful...' Henry was right; life was noisy and mad most times, but at least I had a home. *Used to* have a home...

'I didn't mean that.' Henry leant forward and touched my arm. 'W-what I meant was... I mean, George and... I know we're very different, Hope, but in truth you've got friends, excitement, freedom! What I'd give to be free.'

'Not out of choice!' I pulled my arm away. 'Friends? Who'd sell you for a shilling! Excitement, yeah, until the peelers get hold of you. Then there's no freedom neither.'

I thought about my real pa, who was dead near on five years. He'd planned to take us to America, where there were real opportunities for hard working people like us. Then Ma found out she were expecting the little-uns, and he said he'd work longer shifts to try to save the fare quicker…

'If my pa were still alive, I'd be out of this place. Living on a ranch, with the sun on my face and more horses than London's cabbies own altogether, but healthy and roaming free – not heading for the glue factory. Imagine that, Henry!'

'W-where were you going? America?'

'Yeah. Pa showed me a picture once. "Hope," he said, "With all the money I'll make on the railroad we'll be rich. We'll live on a ranch and have horses. And just think – fresh air."'

'W-what happened?'

'A bridge he was working on collapsed and…' I couldn't bear to think about it. 'Pa died, along with his two best friends.'

'I'm sorry.' Henry rubbed at his shorn head. 'Is it really horrid… I mean, for you…? Home and everything?'

'It in't always bad. Even after Albert came. And then he changed – started hitting Ma. Drinking all his wages.' I stopped. I could feel everything pouring out of me and I was afraid I'd lose control. 'You know, Henry, your pa, I mean Mac, he said I could train to be a nurse. They need women to mend the soldiers – in war.' I thought about Mac… If only Henry had gotten to know his pa. I could feel myself about to cry, but I held it in. 'You know, Henry, me and you in't that different – we're just two restless souls trying to find meaning in this miserable world.'

Henry moved closer. 'I'll help you, Hope. I promise I will. You'll never have to go back to that place, not if you don't want to.'

'That's what your pa said. And then he went and died. I don't want *you* to die, Henry.' I could hardly speak, but the words just kept coming, even though I tried to stop.

Henry put his arm around my shoulder. 'I w-won't die, Hope. And I won't let you down. If you help me stop Xavier and your pa blackmailing Nana, I'll be able to look after you, and your sisters.'

This was the first time Henry had promised to care for my sisters. The tears were stinging my eyes; I rubbed my face and tried to hide the truth from Henry. But in the end it all just came out…

'Pa said that an auction would get the best price. And Ma said I was old enough. Old enough for what, I says? "You'll find out," she says, "we might as well get paid, as give you away for nothing." I told her I in't ready. But Ma in't having none of it. "None of us ever are, Hope," she says, "and Albert in't waiting no longer – he'll get a good price if you go now." So it felt like a miracle when your pa turned up, looking like a gent what lost his way. Ma pulled him off the street and says to Pa, "Looks like we have a prime turkey here – just right for the plucking, perfect for our Hope." I guessed even then they must've been making plans. Only now, with Mac gone…seems I'm fair game. So the auction it is…'

'Auction?'

I was ashamed to go on. But if I wanted Henry's help, I'd have to tell him. 'Pa's put me up for sale!'

'You! W-why? I don't understand. It's against the law…'

'No. You wouldn't… How could you? There's one law for you toffs, and a different one for the likes of me, Henry. Anyways it's too late now 'cause I in't never going back and that's it.'

'Hope… I'm sorry. If—'

'Henry, this in't about me. I promised Mac. And I keep my promises…'

102

Henry didn't speak for ages – I guessed he was thinking about his pa.

'Tell me about my father, Hope. What was he like?'

'Mac, I mean your pa, was goodness itself. He was sick as a dog when Ma found him; didn't know who he was or where he'd been.' I was frightened to tell Henry the truth, but I had to if I wanted him to trust me. 'Pa says "ideal", and starts rubbing his hands together and jabbering on about getting us out of Cable Street once and for all. I weren't too sure what he meant, but it weren't long before I found out. One way or the other I'd be sold. And your pa was a perfect catch.'

'I'm sorry, Hope.' Henry leant back and pulled his knees up to his chin. He sat like that for a while, not speaking. I wasn't sure whether to tell him about his pa's addiction – after all that was what stopped him from going home. That and the guilt.

'Henry. How much do you really know about your pa?'

'Not much. Like I said before, Father and Mother were forbidden topics.'

'But you must know something. Like what he looked like, or what he liked to do… I don't know – something!'

Henry sat quietly, rocking himself again, back and forth. Without looking up he said, 'He was a lepidopterist…'

'A what?'

'Father collected insects – butterflies mainly.'

'What for?'

'Pinning. Displaying.'

'Pinning – like with pins? That's cruel, that is.'

'I know. Father liked to draw them. And the colours, he loved the colours. I found some of his paintings in the attic once. W-when I asked Nana about them, she said she "couldn't tolerate being reminded of what might've been".'

'But you'd think—'

'I know. But no one spoke about either of my parents. That's how it was – the silence of secrets! If you were a Mackenzie, you'd understand.'

'Oh.'

I wanted to tell Henry how wonderful Mac was to me, how he protected me from Pa. And how he'd often talked about his family after one of his night sweats. But I was afraid; afraid that Henry might hate me for being close to his father. And I needed Henry to like me more than ever, now that Ma had thrown me out.

'What do you think is in the letters?' The way Henry stood up and dusted the dirt off his trousers, you'd think he still had his tweed suit on. 'It must be something awful if Xavier thinks he can blackmail Nana.'

'Not sure… Could be anything. I mean, your pa was ill. Maybe he needed money for his medicine.'

'How is that scandalous?'

'There's more than one kind of medicine, Henry! Your pa was in pain, in his head… He needed something to help him… I'm sorry. Opium seemed to work.'

'Are you telling me that my father smoked opium?'

'I'm just… He was getting better, Henry. I swear. Mac was… He'd practically stopped, Henry. That's why his dying from it seems so…'

'So what?'

'Suspicious.' There, I'd said it. 'It makes me think that maybe your pa was—' Henry didn't let me finish; he pushed his way out from under the tree and hurried off towards the street, covering his ears.

'Murdered!' I shouted after him.

# THE ORIENTAL CLUB

# 22

**Henry**

Walking back towards the club, I thought about what Hope had said. Could Xavier have murdered his own brother? Maybe the letters would prove it, one way or the other. I thought about Nana and what she'd say if she saw me now. Which made me smile, thinking of her reaction if she passed by me on the street looking like this. But then I realised she wouldn't even recognise me, probably wouldn't look at me twice – and Jones our footman would more than likely shoo me out of his way. I'd be invisible – like Hope, George, Crooner and Tosher.

As we neared The Oriental, I heard a whistle; I ignored it at first as I thought it was a nearby bird. But Hope recognised George's signal and nipped behind a wall near to the club.

'That-Xavier-geezer-has-just-left,' George said in a rush, as if it was one word. 'Elsie-said-we've-only-ten-minutes.' He grabbed me by the arm, and took me to one side. 'Right-Henry, you-can't-come, it's-too-risky-see.' George took a deep breath and slowed down a little. 'Hope will be quicker, and she knows the hiding place if we have to make a run for it. You stick with

Tosher and Crooner.' Then, addressing the whole group, George said, 'We're relying on you lot to give the signal – if anyone looks as if they're heading our way, you know what to do…'

'W-what?' I asked, feeling left out. 'I don't know what to do.'

'Run!' They all answered at the same time, which started them laughing, like it was the funniest thing anyone had ever said. Despite my fear of being caught and failing to get the letters, their filthy faces and their devil-may-care attitude made me laugh too.

'All right,' said Hope. 'It's agreed. We haven't much time, so let's get going. If we're not back soon, you head back to Jacob's and wait.'

George started pacing around; he looked really nervous. 'Yeah, and if we gets caught, on my h-onour I won't squeal.' George put his hand over his heart. 'You can be sure on that.' Then, looking at me, he said, 'Promise me, Henry, that you'll look after the boys if I gets thrown in clink.'

'That w-won't…' I started to reassure him. 'After all, it's only my uncle, Xavier, I'm sure—'

Hope cut me off. 'Sorry, Henry. That's exactly why… Xavier will have contacts – in with the Beaks, for sure. If we gets caught, it'll be the workhouse or gaol. Either way, promise me you'll look after Tosher and Crooner, and my little sisters.'

I felt the whole thing was being blown out of proportion. I thought I should just march into the club and tell Xavier that I knew about his plans and that I wanted the letters. What could he do? If he tried anything I would tell Nana and the Metropolitan Police would arrest him. But for some reason I felt cautious. 'I promise,' I said, putting my hand over my heart too. 'Whatever happens, I'll make sure they're all looked after.'

Hope and George seemed happy with my promise and ran off in the opposite direction to the club's entrance; I guessed they must've known a secret way in, probably to avoid the porters – which, George had said earlier, were really hired muscle in suits.

'Right,' said Tosher, taking the lead. 'I'll hide behind that tree there…' He pointed to a cluster of silver birch trees opposite the entrance. 'Crooner, you head on down a bit towards The Strand, and if you see anything suspicious – like that Xavier geezer heading back this way – you gets back here as fast as your legs can carry you.'

'W-where shall I go?' I said, although I could already sense Tosher's answer.

'You stay here. When all's safe, we'll come get you.'

'That's not fair.' I was beginning to get fed up with being treated like an infant. I was head and shoulders taller than Hope and George, and, although the boys were my height, I figured they must be a lot younger. 'It's my problem, not yours. The letters, the blackmail, Xavier! It's my life that's falling apart and I want to do something!'

'You are doing something. What are we all here for if we in't doing nothing?' Tosher ran across the street and disappeared behind the trees, and before I had chance to argue, Crooner vanished too.

I stood staring at the front entrance to the club – the gentlemen's club that I'd soon be a member of, if Xavier had his way. The club that protected Xavier and other aristocrats from scandal, but had failed to protect my father. A rather large porter marched up and down in front of the building, like a sentry on duty. Every now and then he stopped and took something out of his pocket, which he drank from – I supposed it was coffee to keep himself alert. Although it was May, the air was chilly; the smog that cloaked everything in the city was hanging ominously above the treetops.

Discretion obviously wasn't Tosher's strong point, as I could see him peeking out from behind the trees. I hoped that the porter had better things to think on than some gangly boy acting strange. It felt as if time was standing still, waiting for something to happen, or for George and Hope to reappear. A couple of police constables strolled by and the porter doffed his hat and stood to attention.

# THE SEARCH

# 23

**Hope**

We finally got in through the servants' door. Everyone seemed to be elsewhere, which was good. I couldn't see Elsie though, and she was supposed to meet us and let us in. Now what were we going to do? On the first floor of the building there were at least half a dozen possible rooms.

'Where's Elsie? I thought she was going to be here?' I asked George.

'How do I know? I in't her keeper.'

'What we going to do then?' I was terrified we'd get spotted and have to tell Henry we'd failed. Everything depended on me getting the letters. If Henry had to do it himself then he wouldn't need me and my plans of a better life would be over.

'Listen, George, best we split up. You take the top rooms. I'll check the bottom.' I pointed to the hidden stairwell, which must've been the service stairs. 'If you get stopped, just act like you're an imbecile, and got lost or something.' George pulled a face and ran off in the direction of the staircase.

With George gone, I looked over the bannister to see if anyone had heard us, but everything was quiet. The silence in the club was eerie. It was as if The Oriental was completely separate to the rest of London.

I crept downstairs and over to the first door to listen; I could hear someone talking but not clearly enough to work out what was being said. The next room had an oil lamp burning; the light flickered underneath the door. Someone must've been in the room, as no one in their right mind would leave a lighted lamp. I moved on to the room at the end, which was in complete darkness and deadly silent. I tried the doorknob – the room was locked. I wondered whether to knock, just in case, but time was running out.

As I tried to jimmy the lock, George leant over the railings above and said, 'I've searched one room – nothing. There's a geezer in one, and I can't seem to get the door to shift on this last one. What do you want me to do?'

'Shh!' I said. 'Come here and help me.'

Just as I managed to get the lock to click open, George appeared carrying a leather purse. 'Where did you get that? You said you didn't find nothing!' I pulled George into the room and closed the door behind us.

'I meant letters— There weren't no letters! But there's at least five pounds—'

'George. We in't here to steal money – you'll get the peelers after us. You'll have to put it back.'

'I in't. And you can't make me. Me and the boys in't had a proper dinner in weeks.'

'Damn it.' I didn't have time to argue. 'Listen, you search the drawers and I'll look over here.' I started pulling the books off the shelves and flapping them open to see if anything fell out.

'How many letters are there?' asked George.

'I in't sure. But when Mac asked me to make sure I got them to Henry, he showed me a bundle about this big.' I held my hand up to show George the size. 'And they were tied together with green string.'

We both swept through the room in no time, and found nothing.

'Now what?' George was pushing the bottom drawer back into the dresser when I heard a voice outside.

'Have you packed my bags, Elsie? The coach leaves at seven thirty sharp.'

'I was just about to do it, sir.' Elsie's voice seemed a little shaky. 'If you like, I can fetch you when I'm done.'

'What have you been doing, girl? I asked you to do it for six thirty. Do I have to do everything myself?'

'I'm sorry, sir, it weren't my fault, honest.'

George was pointing at the window and beckoning me to climb out with him. I tried to mouth that I needed to find the letters – that he should go and I'd wait to see if Elsie managed to get Xavier away from the room. George shook his head and came over to me by the door.

'At least we know it's this Xavier geezer's room,' he whispered.

'The letters must be here then,' I said.

Elsie was trying hard to stop Xavier from entering the room; I could hear her pleading with him.

'Please, sir, if the porter finds out I didn't do as you asked I'll be whipped and I'll lose my job.'

'I won't tell the porter, Elsie. Don't worry.'

The keys rattled in the lock. I dived under the bed and George hid behind a curtain that led to a small washroom. I crawled to the bottom of the bed so I could get a better look at the door. As I reached out to pull the blanket down over the bed's end, my hand caught on something between the mattress and the wooden slats. The letters!

As Elsie pleaded with Xavier, I pulled the bundle of letters from their hiding place.

'Psst, George?' I whispered.

'What?'

'I've got the letters!' I stuck my head out from under the bed; George was peeking out from behind the curtain. 'When Xavier comes in, you distract him by making some commotion and I'll make a run for it.'

'All right,' said George. 'I'll see you back at the den.'

# THE TRUTH – PART ONE

# 24

**Henry**

I was starting to get anxious waiting for Hope, and had decided to go up to the porter and demand to be shown to Xavier's rooms, when Hope came running past the porter and out into the street.

'Got them. Come on...' Hope swept past Tosher who was quick to follow. I looked back towards the club, but I couldn't see George. The porter looked at Hope and Tosher, and then headed back into the building. There seemed to be a lot of shouting, but I couldn't hear who was saying what. A young girl hurried out of the building, holding the side of her face, crying and mumbling to herself. I was pretty sure it was George's girl, Elsie, but as far as I knew, it could've been a trap. Hope and Tosher were disappearing fast into the distance, so, as soon as the porter was out of view, I chased after them.

I caught up with Hope and Tosher near Blackfriars Bridge. 'W-where's George?' I shouted. Hope and Tosher were ahead of me by a few feet. Neither answered. As we got to the other side of the river Hope stopped and looked back.

'I think your uncle has him.' Hope was leaning forward, breathing heavily, her hands on her knees.

'W-what? H-how?'

'You left George?' Tosher wasn't impressed. 'I thought we were in this together?'

'We are, Tosher, but George told me to run. I was—'

'You still shouldn't've left him. What if the peelers get him?' Tosher was pacing back and forth, thumping his fist into his hand. I had to admit I was shocked that Hope had left him, for all her talk of friendship and sticking together.

'I agree with Tosher. W-we can't leave George; we should go back.'

'You gone mad?' Hope was already heading off towards Jacob's. 'George in't stupid – he knew what he was doing. Come on…'

I looked at Tosher. 'If George isn't back by dusk I'll go to the police and explain. I won't let him take the blame. I promise.'

Tosher seemed to relax a little. 'All right, spit on it.' And for the second time I went through the little ritual, which seemed to be as binding as a military oath.

As we walked back towards Jacob's, Tosher separated himself from me and Hope, as though he was lost without his companions.

'Where are the letters?' I said to Hope, desperate to see them.

'In my satchel – they'll be all right until we get back. Now's not the place to stop; your uncle could already have the peelers after us.'

Hope was right of course, but I so wanted to read my father's letters. I had a strange feeling in my stomach, scared of what I might find out.

'How many letters are there?' I asked.

'Well, I didn't count them – sort of otherwise occupied, wasn't I?' Hope held her hand up and separated her thumb and forefinger. 'About this many altogether.'

The distance was about one and a half inches. 'That must mean about fifteen or twenty letters, at least.'

'We'll find out in a minute if you get a move on.'

Hope started running again, and Tosher was right on her heels. I felt exhausted, and excited, but also terrified of what I might or might not learn about my family. I tried to keep up with them both but the damn shoes I'd exchanged at Mr Arnold's were ill-fitting and kept slipping off. It was a wonder I didn't turn an ankle or something. As we neared Jacob's Island, the now familiar stench of the river and raw sewage stung my eyes and caught at the back of my throat. It was literally unbearable. All the houses, if you could call them that, were made of timber, which was rotting away with the residents in them. Each narrow footbridge and gangway was nothing more than a plank or two of soaking wet, slime-covered oak. I realised that if I got separated from Hope or the boys I'd never find my way out of this hellhole.

After following the route back through the rooms and corridors into the den, Hope threw herself on the floor. She was panting and sweating and quite red in the face. 'That was close,' she said, her voice shaky. 'I'm sure George will be all right. He's always all right.'

'Let's hope so,' said Tosher. 'And where's Crooner?'

Hope didn't answer. I supposed she didn't know. Within minutes Tosher was sitting in the corner of the room, silently tying and untying a piece of string. His silence was oppressive. I felt as though he was blaming me in some way for the loss of his friend and leader, which I supposed was right. And even Hope, who usually never stopped talking, was hushed, deep in thought.

'Can I see the letters, please?' I held out my hand to Hope, who was sitting with the satchel on her lap.

'I pray they'll help you, Henry, honest-to-God I do.'

Hope handed me the bundle of letters. They were tied in green string as Hope had said they were, but they'd obviously been opened and roughly thrown back together. I wasn't comfortable with reading the letters with Hope and Tosher in the room, but they'd risked so much to help me, I felt if I said anything I'd sound ungrateful and selfish.

'I'nt you goin' to read them then?' Hope was leaning back, looking up at me. 'Or do you want some privacy, like?'

Hope was trying to be tactful and kind, but she made me feel under pressure, like I should sit down with her and Tosher and spill my unknown life out on the floor between us.

'I w-would prefer to be alone – if you don't mind, that is.'

'Come on, Tosh,' said Hope. 'Let's go and see if we can find George, and pick some grub up on the way. Might even bump into Crooner...'

After Hope and Tosher left, I sat on the pile of old sacking near the broken window and started to read the letters. I was keen to know what was in them that could make my nana a victim of blackmail. And I was desperate to know more about my father; hopefully I'd find out why he hadn't come home after Afghanistan.

I counted the letters out; there were eighteen in total, one written almost every month since August 1849. Every envelope had the same address – my home in Belgravia. For some reason my father must've decided not to post any of them. Probably the same reason he hadn't returned home. I decided to start with the oldest letter; that way I would gain more of a sense of him, and his state of mind. I took all the letters out of the envelopes and worked my way through them. I tried desperately not to be drawn in and read the letters out of order. It was really hard, as every now and then I'd catch a word: 'mother', 'missing', 'lonely', 'madness', 'Henry'. The sound of my father saying my name ran

**116**

through my mind. I was sure I could hear him laughing and calling out my name: 'Henry, Henry, Henry.'

*15th August 1849*
*Cable Street*
*Whitechapel*

*Dearest Henry,*

*My darling son, I hardly know where to start.*

*The beginning is usually the best place, or so I've heard. So I will try to explain to you why I'm unable to return home at this time. It's hard to remember the detail, as I'm still very sick and struggling to accept what has happened to me and what I've become.*

*You must be a young man now – fourteen, fifteen? So I hope what I say is comprehensible to you. I apologise, Henry, for not remembering your birth date, but I've blocked much from my mind, that which I don't wish to remember, but sadly it has taken many happy, good memories too. All I know is that I'm in London, and that the landlady has tasked her daughter to take care of me. I'm told I'm currently living in Cable Street, which is a fairly grim place, truly. But I'm not in a position to be choosy and I'm grateful for the care I'm given.*

*Hope, the landlady's daughter, says her 'ma' found me wandering the streets and took me in. I have some property of value, which is enough to see me through for a while. It's only been during the last few weeks that I've remembered who I am – for years I was completely ignorant of my heritage and family. But I'm not fit to return home. Not yet. I will soon though, God willing.*

*Sorry, Henry, I'll have to leave it for now. I'm exhausted. I will write again before long, I promise.*

*I truly hope and pray that this letter finds you in good health. May God be with you and bless you.*

*With infinite love,*

*Your dearest father*

August 1849! I couldn't believe that Father's letter was near on two years old, and that he'd been living in London all that time, not far from his home. Not far from me.

I read several letters – most of the which were rambling and I could tell that Father must've found some days more difficult than others. In some of the letters, Father had written but a single sentence; sometimes he'd drawn a picture. But not one of the letters I'd read so far had mentioned my mother, or anything that'd warrant someone believing they could make money out of my family. Then I found two letters tucked inside one another – they were brief and in a different hand to my fathers'…

*The Oriental*
*18 Hanover Square*
*London*

*Henry. Brother. There's no other way to say this. I seem to have gotten myself into some difficulty at the club. I need your help. I have kept your secret for two years now. And now I need you to keep mine – I have lost Mother's house at cards. I cannot believe it myself. But there it is. I need you to release £10,000 pounds from your inheritance. I know this means you will have to come home and you were against it. But really, Henry, I have no one else to turn to. I promise that your past will forever remain a secret with me – Mother need never know about your opium use, or where you currently reside.*

*Xavier*

The second letter was even shorter…

*I am desperate, Henry. Please come home. I never planned to tell you this – but you leave me no option. I have some news about Emma, and with Mother so ill…you need to come home and face your responsibilities. I will arrange to collect you.*

*Xavier*

So that was it. Xavier had been behind the whole thing! And what was the news Xavier had regarding my mother?

The letter Hope gave me after the exhibition suggested that my mother was alive – could it be true? Now I knew why Father didn't mention her in any of his previous letters to me – he didn't know himself. Xavier had kept it from Father, until he was needed!

When Hope returned she brought some cold meatloaf and two apples she'd found. 'Must've fallen out of someone's basket,' she said.

I wasn't in the mood for eating so I told Hope to give my share to the boys. Crooner and Tosher didn't need to be told twice and ate the food greedily.

'No luck in finding George?' I was worried about him and knew that until he turned up, the boys would be on edge.

'We think the peelers 'ave 'im,' said Tosher, through a mouthful of apple. 'We went back to The Oriental, and that fat porter was still on guard. Crooner went up and asked about Elsie. He said, "She don't work here – now clear off before I get the law on you."'

'So w-what w-will we do n-now?' It was starting to get dark and I really didn't want to spend the night in Jacob's Island – after all, hadn't Henry Mayhew reported in *The Times* that 'a poor man would murder his own mother for a scrap of bread' here.

# THE BEGINNING OF THE END

# 25

**Hope**

I'd been lying curled up on the floor, pretending to be asleep since daylight. The boys had gone roaming after Henry had finally fallen asleep. They said they were going to find George. I didn't blame them; hanging around doing nothing was worse than just waiting for bad news to come knocking.

'Henry, are you awake?' I whispered. No answer. I got up as quietly as I could; I needed a Jimmy Riddle and I didn't want spectators. The floor creaked as I crossed the room. I stopped, waiting to see if Henry would wake up. No, still fast asleep on his bed of sacks. The rats had been running around us all night, so I'd tried to stay awake and keep watch over the little bread we'd left, but they'd got to it anyway. All that was left was the kerchief the bread had been wrapped in, with a few more holes to show the rats had been.

'Hope?' Henry sat up and stretched. 'W-where're you going?'

'Um. Nowhere.'

'W-where are the boys?'

'Gone off to find George. Or at least get some particulars on his whereabouts.'

'Oh.' Henry pulled the bundle of letters from under the sacking. Thank God the rats hadn't got them.

'Did you find much out? From the letters, like?' I asked.

'Not so far – nothing useful anyhow.' Henry opened one of them. 'This letter, dated February 1851, says, "Xavier called to see me. The news about Mother disturbed me greatly, Henry. If only I had known…" Then he goes off on a tangent, rambling about the music halls and singing. But he doesn't say what news, or how and when he found out, whatever it was he found out.'

'Maybe there's more letters somewhere?'

'Possibly. But the letter you gave me, which was Father's final letter, still didn't elaborate. And I don't understand Xavier visiting. If he knew Father was in that p-place, why didn't he tell us?'

I felt sorry for Henry in a way. Despite all his wealth, he was still alone in the world, just like the rest of us.

'He must've had a reason, Henry – not to tell, I mean. Do you think if you went back now to your grandma's she would tell you the truth? I mean, you've the letters to show her – surely she wouldn't hide the facts now, would she?'

'I'm not sure. I've come so far to risk it, Hope.' Henry placed the letters carefully back under the sacks, as if the coarse hemp was silk sheeting. 'I don't want to be deceived; I want the truth, not some half-hearted, romantic story to keep me happy.'

'Like I said before, Henry, sometimes it's for the best.'

I didn't really believe what I was saying; it weren't always for the best. Henry was right – people always seem to say what they think you *should* hear, or what they think you *want* to hear. And if Henry's family sent him off to school, he may never know the truth about his pa and ma.

'Listen, Henry; if you stay here, I'll go and get something to eat. It'll give you time to finish reading your letters. You might discover something, like. And if the boys come back, tell them to wait here.'

I hurried out of the den before Henry could argue.

*

It paid to have contacts in Jacob's, although I wouldn't have called them *friends* exactly. It was ev'ryman for 'imself in the end, for all of us. But if there weren't no quarrel, then you could trust most of them with your life. I'd gone in search of food, but decided kind of last minute to drop in on Aunt Sal to see if she'd heard anything about George. Sal weren't really my aunt, but I'd always called her that.

I was glad I did drop by, 'cause Sal, who did the laundry for all the cathouses around and about, knew all the tittle-tattle, and told me, 'George has been let off, 'cause the peelers didn't have nothing on him. More hassle than it was worth.'

I still had some brass in my satchel from the sale of Henry's suit so, as I hurried back to the den from Aunt Sal's, I picked up two large hot potatoes from Paddy's cart. I hoped George would be back when I got there, but Henry was still alone.

'I've got some food, and some good news. George is free!'

'That's good,' said Henry, not even looking at me.

'Well, you don't seem happy about it,' I said, feeling really annoyed. We'd all put ourselves at risk for Henry and all he could say was 'that's good'!

'I've read all the letters again.' Henry handed me the bundle, all tied together neatly. 'M-mother's in an asylum.'

'Asylum? How? Why?' I didn't know what to say; Mac never said nothing about no madhouse. 'Are you sure?'

'Of course I'm damn sure! It's obvious – am I an idiot too?' Henry thumped the wall he'd been leaning against.

'I didn't mean that. What I meant was—'

122

'*Cage – locked up – trapped!* I don't know how I hadn't worked it out before. My father is dead, Hope. My mother's God-knows-where. Don't you understand?' Henry scratched at his head frantically, as if struggling to clear his thoughts. 'My uncle's t-trying to ruin the family, Hope. And the only person in the world I have left is dying!'

Henry had been crying; there were dirty streaks down his face. 'Henry, listen…' I held out my hand and touched him lightly on the shoulder; he pulled away and faced the wall. 'You have me,' I said, moving closer. 'I know I'm not much, but I'll look out for you, Henry, honest I will.' Henry didn't answer; he just stood with his back to me in silence. In the distance I could hear the tall ships coming up the river, the sailors calling out as they readied to dock. Henry shrugged me off.

'The potatoes will go cold,' I said, sitting down. 'You need to eat.' I unwrapped the steaming potatoes; the thought of the soft, creamy middles made my mouth water. 'Starving yourself to death in't going to change nothing, Henry.' I pulled one of the potatoes apart and started to pick at the burnt, crispy skin whilst the mushy insides cooled.

After a minute or two Henry sat down next to me. 'I'm sorry, Hope. I just feel so alone…' He picked up the other potato and started eating. 'I don't know what to do next.' As Henry ate he tried to stifle his sobs, swallowing deeply through every mouthful.

'I guess we go to the madhouse,' I said. 'When George and the boys get back we'll work somethin' out. Someone will know someone who works there. You'll see.'

# AN ENEMY IN THE CAMP

## 26

**Hope**

When George arrived with the boys in tow he looked as though he'd been dragged through a hedge backwards but, typical of George, he still had a grin on his face.

'Hope, didn't you say that toe rag Jasper was working for Henry's uncle?'

'Yeah. Why?'

'We just saw him, didn't we?' George turned to Tosher and Crooner for confirmation. 'He was asking questions here about. We had to go miles out of our way, we did, to avoid the creep.'

'Oh no, he must've been sent by Xavier. The sooner we get out of here the better.' Henry got up and gathered his bundle of letters. 'It seems my mother is in an asylum, and I'm going to find out why.'

'What, Bedlam? That's where the nut—' I elbowed Tosher in the ribs. 'Ow, that hurt,' he said, rubbing his side. 'What you do that for?'

'Henry wants us to help find his mother,' I said. 'And, when we do – if they won't let her go – we'll break her out.'

'You're all around the bend! If you think that I'm going near *that* madhouse, *they* should lock *you* up and throw away the key.' Tosher pretended to throw something out of the boarded-up window.

'None of you need come if you don't want to.' Henry hurried towards the door. 'But I'm going.'

'You can't go alone, Henry.' I picked up my satchel and held out my hand towards Henry. 'Give me the letters – you don't want to lose them now.'

Henry handed me the bundle of letters. I shoved them in my satchel, next to the sketchbook and knife. But Henry held onto his pa's pocket watch. 'Let's go.'

George was leaning against the wall, biting his fingernails, deep in thought. 'Hang on a minute,' he said. 'Have either of you thought how you're going to get into a place like Bedlam?'

Henry looked at me and shrugged.

I turned to George. 'No point in asking me.' I might've been a bit nifty with jimmying a door lock, but I didn't have a clue where Bedlam was, let alone how to get into the place. I'd heard talk, like everyone else, and most people feared of going anywhere near, just in case. Tosher was right; if anyone was fool enough to try to get inside, then it served them right if they got themselves locked in and experimented on.

'What if we all go, and when we get close enough, we can decide how we'll get in.' George was always willing to have a go; that was why I went to him for help.

Tosher didn't seem convinced, and Crooner stuck with his brother, no matter what. 'Thing is, it in't that we're scared or nothing. It's just Crooner here –' Tosher thumped his brother's arm – 'has an aversion to hospitals. It's our poor mother, and all, he just can't take it.'

'Oh, shut up, Tosh.' George had obviously heard Tosher's story before. 'You didn't even know your *poor mother* – she abandoned you both at the workhouse door!'

'Like I said,' said Henry. 'You've all done so much for me already. I'm sure I could find the p-place, if you just show me which way to go.'

'Don't be daft, Henry,' I said. 'You don't get rid of me that easy.'

Henry smiled, and gave me a hug. 'Thank you.'

'Tosher and Crooner, you might as well stay around here,' said George. 'And if that blabbermouth Jasper comes calling, give him what for.' George handed something to Tosher, which he quickly shoved in his pocket.

'Sure thing, George.' The twins were relieved to stay behind; they said they'd find George if anything happened.

'Come on then…' I said, shoving Henry forward. 'The sooner we get out of here, the less likely we'll bump into Jasper.'

The journey back was difficult. A hole had appeared in the middle of the footbridge, which meant we all had to creep around the outside. You could see right down to the river. Just as well the tide was in – a person might have had a chance in the water.

Jacob's was busier than usual; even the bridges and terraces were overcrowded – something must've been going on. As we hurried along one of the rickety ledges, I asked an old man who was lying around outside the front door of a house why it was so busy.

'Place is crawlin' with peelers. That do-gooder Mayhew is showin' his pal Dickens around.' The man tugged at Henry's shirt. 'Spare a crust, mister?'

Henry pulled away, almost losing his balance. 'S-sorry, I d-don't have any food.' Henry looked at me. 'We'll bring something back though. Won't we, Hope?'

The man tried to get up, but when he couldn't he started mumbling to himself. 'Thinks we're exhibits in some freak show, so he does. Mayhew, bah.'

I looked at Henry and shrugged. We'd be lucky if we got enough food for ourselves, let alone every Tom, Dick and Harry on Jacob's.

'Hurry up!' George pushed his way through and ran on ahead. 'We in't got all day.' Henry started to run after George. Just as I was about to catch up, Henry suddenly stopped dead.

'It's Jasper!' Henry pointed across the makeshift bridge. 'He's found us. Now w-what?'

'Scarper!' said George.

Before I got a chance to say where or what, Henry slipped over the edge and hit the water like a stone.

'Help!' yelled Henry, splashing manically. 'I can't—'

With that, Henry went under.

# A WATERY END
# 27

**Henry**

The water went up my nose, stinging like an open wound. It poured down my throat, despite me trying to keep my mouth shut. I was swallowing the excrement of London. I fought like I'd never fought before, but I couldn't get my head above the surface. I couldn't see anything; it was as if my eyes had been sealed shut. I could hear pounding in my ears – droning on, drumming as though my ears might explode. Someone was calling me: 'Henry, Henry. Hang on, we're cominggggg…' But I couldn't hang on. I kicked and splashed, but I just sank deeper and deeper. I wanted to just let go and fall to the bottom and sleep forever. I thought of my poor mother waiting for me to come and rescue her, trapped, hoping, praying that someone would come at any moment, but who never did. I wanted to tell her that I tried to find her, but not to worry about me; I would be with Father now. As I sank down to the bottomless river, I thought about who'd look after Mother with Father dead and Nana and me… I thought about Xavier; with me and Father out of the way, all his troubles would be over. I bet he'd be laughing now. And what about Hope? Would anyone

128

believe her if she took the letters to the magistrate? Then the voice again…

'Henry! Henry! Grab this!'

The thought of my mother in that awful place gave me strength I didn't know I had; I had to save her. I kicked at the thick muddy water with all my might. I could see a faint light on the surface, a shadow cutting through it. Was I dying? Was this it? Was my father's spirit coming to get me?

'Henry!'

An arm plunged into the sludge. I tried to get a grip. Missed. Again the arm grabbed at me. Again I failed to touch even the fingertips – then a hand touched my arm. I thrashed about, then someone reached down and gripped my wrist. Pulling on my arm, tugging me upwards, the water swirling, me splashing, I could feel myself losing consciousness…

'Henry! Can you hear me?'

I could hear Hope's voice, but I couldn't see her.

'Do you think he's dead?' I didn't recognise who was speaking. I tried to open my eyes, to move my body. I wanted whoever it was to know I was alive.

Hope started crying. She'd never cried in front of me before; she was always so tough. I wanted her to know I was all right. Someone thumped me on the back, and was moving me around – thumping, turning, thumping…

'For God's sake!' I managed to splutter, as I coughed up thick watery liquid. 'I'm all right.'

'Thank God,' the unknown voice said. 'At least I didn't jump in that sewer for nothin'.'

I forced open my eyes, only to see a cloudy Jasper, George and Hope all staring down at me.

'But?' I tried to speak, to make sense of everything. Hadn't we been running from this Jasper boy? And he'd caught up with us anyway.

'You need to get cleaned up, Henry.' Hope was tugging at my arm. 'Come on, we'll go to Aunt Sal's; she'll sort you out.'

'What about him,' I said, pointing at Jasper. 'Uncle Xavier, the let—'

Hope cut me off. 'It's a long story. But we need to get those clothes off you before you get sick. Jasper too.'

George and Jasper pulled me up and carried me by crossing their arms underneath my body. I put my arms around their necks and held on tight, as the boys ran across the footbridges and ledges, slipping and sliding. Hope was shouting for them to slow down and to be careful. I felt disorientated, as if the world was whirling around me, spinning me upside down, forward and backwards.

'Stop!' I shouted, as the contents of my stomach rose within me. As the boys came to a halt, I fell on the floor and vomited all over Hope's feet.

'Disgusting!' Jasper turned away.

'Here, use this.' George took off his neckerchief and threw it at me.

I looked at Hope. Surely she wasn't expecting me to wipe her feet? 'W-what, me?' All three stood and watched, waiting for me to do something. I picked up the cloth and wiped most of the fluid away. 'That's the best I can do,' I said, feeling as if I was about to repeat the action.

'The sooner we get to Sal's the better we'll all be,' said Hope, rubbing her feet on the backs of her legs. 'Come on.'

The boys went to pick me up again.

'I think I'll be better off walking,' I said. The thought of swaying in their makeshift hammock was too much. Then I remembered Father's watch. I checked my shirt pocket. The watch was gone!

*

'Sal?' shouted Hope as we neared one of the warehouses that towered above the rickety buildings we'd left behind. 'Sal? It's Hope.'

A large woman appeared from a doorway; she looked as if she'd never been without food in her life.

'What do you want? Bringing this bunch of thieving good-for-nothings to my door.'

Aunt Sal wiped her hands on her apron and grabbed Hope by the shoulders, pulling her tight to her enormous bosom. It was a wonder she didn't suffocate.

'Hope! What in the world happened?' Sal held Hope at arm's length, inspecting her carefully.

'Henry here gone and fell in the river, didn't he?' Hope shoved me forward like I was some specimen to be examined too.

'Sorry,' I said. 'I didn't mean to. It's just—'

'Of course you didn't…' Aunt Sal took hold of my shirtsleeve and pulled me into the warehouse. 'Come on. Let's see what we can do.'

The washroom was steaming hot; sheets and clothing were hanging from lines strung between hooks, wall to wall. How anyone could get bed linen to look so white and clean in this place was nothing short of a miracle.

Aunt Sal ladled out pints of the boiling soapy water into a metal bath. 'Here, you lot wait over there.' She pointed to an enormous sheet that dripped into a hole in the floor. 'Ladies first. Here, get out of those clothes, Hope.' Hope started to remove her shawl, then her dress. We all stood there staring. 'Move!' shouted Sal, giving George a push. 'Can't a girl have no privacy?'

George shoved Jasper in the back. 'Nothing to look at here, boys.' And reluctantly we shuffled behind the makeshift curtain.

I could hear Hope whispering something to Sal, and the rustle of her clothes. I strained my ears, but they must've still been clogged with mud, as I couldn't quite make out her words.

'What did she say?' I asked.

'Dunno,' said George.

Jasper sat on the floor and started to remove his boots, then his shirt. 'I'm next,' he said. 'I in't going in after you…' Jasper looked at me in disgust. 'God knows how many whoppers you've swallowed.'

George laughed. 'Leave him alone, Jasper.'

'W-what's a w-whopper?'

'You don't wanna know,' said Jasper.

'How did you do that?' Aunt Sal's voice was loud enough to hear back in Belgravia. 'That cut looks infected. Here…'

Hope's reply was too quiet for me to hear. But whatever Aunt Sal did, it made Hope scream out in pain.

When Hope joined us behind the curtain, I hardly recognised her. Her face was positively shining; her hair was wet and twisted into some kind of plait, which hung down her back. The clothes she had on were torn and raggedy, but at least they were clean. Hope was still barefoot.

'Next,' Aunt Sal called.

Hope pushed me in front of Jasper. 'Henry's next. You've waited this long for a wash, Jasper, a few more minutes in't going to make no difference.'

'That in't fair. It's me that saved the blighter.'

'That's life, in't it,' moaned George. 'Might as well get used to it.'

And for the second time that day I was plunged underwater.

# The Final Journey

# 28

**Hope**

After Aunt Sal had fed us all, and the boys had finished fighting about who did what to who, we set off, in the direction of Bedlam. Aunt Sal had said it was more than likely Henry's ma was there. For 'posh folks', she'd said. When we'd asked where it was, she'd replied, 'Close to St George's Circus. Near the obelisk – you can't miss it.' I felt real nervous though, as I'd never travelled far from Whitechapel before, and I was worried about where we'd find help if we needed it, not to mention getting caught.

I looked at Henry. He was a real picture; I doubted if his own grandma would recognise him. If I hadn't known where Henry had come from, I'd have easily thought he could be one of us. He was thinner and paler than when we'd first met. And even with Aunt Sal's clean clothes he looked as though he'd spent all his life in the slums; his disguise was far too convincing.

Henry was more worried about having Jasper with us, but as Jasper said, 'If I'd wanted to dob Henry in, why did I bother savin' the git?' He had a point. But Henry still wasn't sure, and neither was George.

'How long do you reckon it'll take?' asked Jasper. 'Only me ma might be wondering where I is.'

'I thought you were wanting to help us out – rescuing Henry's dear mother and all,' said George.

Jasper rubbed at his neck; I figured the clean starched shirt was making him sore. 'I do. I just got to keep me options open, that's all.'

Jasper had told me that Henry's Uncle Xavier was only trying to help Henry, and that's why he'd sent him on the lookout. I didn't wholly believe him; Jasper had a bit of name for being two-sided. But something about Jasper's story felt right, and I was usually fairly good at sussing people out. I decided not to tell Henry – not yet, not till we had real proof one way or the other, but it did put another angle on it.

'George, how do you think we'll get inside?' Henry was coming out of himself a bit more, and I'd noticed his stammer was less too.

'I in't worked it out yet,' said George. 'I 'spect we can distract the officers or something and you and Hope can sneak in whilst there's a commotion.'

'There'll be *o-officers*?' said Henry.

'George don't know that for sure, do you, George?' Jasper looked worried.

'Course he don't,' I said. 'Just worse case, in't it, George?'

The streets were busy with traders, hawkers and young-uns, all begging for a bob or two, but no one bothered us; I guessed they could see we were as hard up as them. George wanted to stop by the Marshalsea to see a friend's pa – he thought he might be able to help us out, as he'd helped people get loved ones out of Bedlam before.

When we got near to St George the Martyr church, George told us to wait in the graveyard whilst he went in. He said the ironmonger didn't like strangers around the place – made him uneasy, like.

'Do you think my mother will still be there, Hope?' Henry sat down on a broken headstone that had fallen over, looking like the whole world was on his shoulders. Jasper was wandering about, looking real nervous. I still weren't convinced about his story, but there was something about what he said that rang true.

'Not sure. Guess we'll find out soon enough.'

It seemed like ages since Henry had turned up on my doorstep. Things had definitely gotten a bit scary at times, 'specially after Henry nearly drowned an' all. There was no going back for me, and I wondered what I'd do once Henry had rescued his ma and saved his grandma from scandal. Where would I fit in the picture? Probably not at all. I was really anxious about going to the madhouse – they said that women got locked away just for having a baby out of wedlock. The place would be full if the authorities had a mind to visit Whitechapel or Seven Dials, not to mention all the other rookeries.

When George came out he was dangling a massive bunch of keys. 'Here, look what I've got! The old geezer has done us proud he has, only copied the keys to the whole damn nuthouse, in't he.'

'Well, don't show the world, George. The peelers might snatch them off us.' I took the bunch of keys from George and put them in my satchel. There must've been at least a dozen or more keys, held together on a large ring. My satchel weighed twice as much with the clanking iron keys in it.

'Blimey, George.' Jasper was quite excited at seeing the keys. He knew it would mean that we wouldn't be forcing no lock or smashing no windows. 'Don't suppose your contact said which key opened what door like?'

'What do you think, you absolute moron?' George shoved Jasper in the chest, making him lose his balance. 'At least half the damn keys look the same—'

'Can you all stop arguing for a minute so I can think?' I was fed up of the boys always trying to outdo one another. The only one that didn't bother was Henry, but I guessed he wasn't sure of us yet – I figured underneath all his poshness, he was probably just the same as George and Jasper.

'Do you know which way to go?' asked Henry.

'Nope,' said George. 'But when we get there we're to ask for a man named Oxford, who, according to my source, has the most knowledge of all about the inmates. More important, he knows your Ma!'

'Eh? How could he…' Henry looked shocked. 'I don't understand…'

'You will,' said George. 'C'mon, I think it's this way.' George pointed across the graveyard and through the church. 'Unless you're a ghost though, we gotta walk around the building, in't we?' George walked on ahead, turning now and then to make sure we were all still following. Jasper ran to catch George up while I hung back with Henry, who'd gone quiet again.

'Look, Henry, if you in't sure we don't have to go.'

Henry looked at me; his pale blue eyes were ringed with red. 'I don't have a choice, Hope. W-who else will save my mother?'

'You always have a choice,' I said. 'We all have a choice, even when it looks like there in't no choice.'

As we cut through Borough Market, Jasper and George split up, one going one way and one the other. I wondered what they were doing, but I soon found out.

'Oi, you, you little…'

'Stop that bleeding thief!'

'He's stolen me husband's sausages…'

George and Jasper flew past me and Henry, and disappeared out of the market the way we'd just come in. Several people were standing around, looking at the market traders as they ran after the boys.

'If I get my bleeding hands on you, you won't know what's hit you,' shouted a young woman with a couple of children at her heels. 'Takin' the food out of the little-uns mouths!'

Henry looked in the direction where the boys had vanished. 'W-why have they gone that way?'

I slipped my arm through Henry's. 'You'll find out,' I said. And I skipped Henry out the opposite side of the market.

When we reached the ob'liss, Jasper and George appeared, smiling like two demented escapees.

'Look.' Jasper held up two steaming hot pies. 'George?'

George opened his shirt and revealed a string of sausages, already cooked, along with a whole round of bread. 'Da-dah!'

Henry clapped his hands and hugged George, then Jasper. 'That's w-wonderful. You're both so clever.'

'Let's find somewhere quiet,' I said. 'We'd best keep out of people's way. You never know who knows what, or who!'

We found a small alleyway that looked as though it was completely abandoned. Apart from a couple of wild dogs digging at the ground, and an old woman lying asleep in the gutter, there wasn't a soul about.

'Here's somewhere…' Jasper pulled a plank of wood from a boarded-up doorway, and then another. A notice was pasted on the side of the building; I tried to work out what it said.

'C-O-N-D, cond, D-E-M, dem, condem—'

'Condemned,' finished Henry. 'It says the building is condemned, and to be demolished.'

'Ah well.' George was already climbing through the gap. 'I doubt it'll be knocked down today.'

137

'But it's probably dangerous,' said Henry, climbing in behind George. 'It could fall down around our ears.'

No one paid any attention though, and within moments the boys had all disappeared inside the building. As I stepped into the space, a blanket of pitch black swallowed my vision. 'Watch your step,' I called into the darkness, almost falling down a hole myself. 'Let's not go too far in.'

'Shut up moaning,' said George. 'You're always distressing about everything.' He sounded miles away.

The building creaked every time someone moved; I couldn't tell who was where. I put my hands out in front of me, feeling for posts, walls, anything. The room felt really cold, as if it'd never seen the light of day.

'Do you think there are any ghosts?' I called into the icy black space. No one answered. 'George? Jasper?' Still no answer. I stopped walking. 'Henry?'

A chill went through me. Ghosts! My heart was pounding in my throat. 'Stop messing about,' I shouted into the darkness. I was frightened to turn around and go back, in case things got worse. 'George?'

I stood still, silent; waiting. Waiting for some sound to show the boys were still in the building. Nothing. Where could they have gone? Maybe they'd all fallen through the floor and were lying dead at the bottom. Maybe they'd run off as a lark and would come back and try to jump out on me. They wouldn't frighten me. I waited, willing my eyes to see through the never-ending blackness.

'I know you're there, Jasper.' No answer.

I stepped forward slowly, testing the floor for holes or unstable planks. Just let them wait till I got my hands on them, leaving me behind. But what if…

'Hope?' The sudden voice in the darkness nearly finished me off. 'Hurry up…' A hand grabbed hold of my ankle and pulled me down towards the floor. 'Down here…' I slipped through the gap in the floor and into the arms of Henry. 'Are you all right? I thought you were behind us…'

# FOOLISHNESS

# 29

**Hope**

The sausages were wonderful. And even though Jasper stuffed a whole pie to himself, saying, *finders, keepers,* George happily shared all he'd got, although Henry, who generally only thought of his belly, didn't seem interested in no food.

'We'd best wait until all the visitors have left,' said George. 'Then when all the officers are busy feeding the luna— I mean, the patients, we'll sneak in and see if we can locate this Oxford bloke.'

'How do you pre-pose we're going to find this par-ticular gent? In a house full of similar gents, I mean.' Jasper was right. None of us knew who this person was, let alone recognise him. Henry had a picture of his ma, but that was drawn years gone by. Suddenly it all felt hopeless.

'W-what did you say this gentleman's name was?' asked Henry.

'Oxford,' said George. 'Why?'

'Well, the name sounds kind of f-familiar.'

'And?'

'Before we went to the exhibition, Nana said something about the man who tried to shoot Queen Victoria. I'm sure *his* name was Oxford. I think there was an article in *The Times*, expressing concerns that there might be another attempt on the Queen's life at the exhibitions opening ceremony.'

Jasper started prancing about with his nose in the air, like a dandy. 'An article in *The Times*, ooh, I say—'

'Jasper! Is everything a comedy to you?' I was starting to regret letting Jasper come along, but I remembered what my ma used to say: 'Best to keep your enemies close.' Real good at giving advice my ma was – not much good at taking it though. And I wasn't sure one way or the other with regards to Jasper.

'The thing is,' said Henry, 'the article said that this fellow, and I'm sure his name was Oxford, was a patient at Bethlem, Bedlam that is. I didn't think twice on it at the time. What if…?' Henry went quiet.

'What if what?' said Jasper. 'And anyways, how will your knowing Oxford's at Bedlam help us any, if we still don't know his identity, like?'

'W-well, apparently he's recovered from his mania, and has become an excellent violin player. *The Times* said his playing calms the patients at Bethlem. There was an illustration too.'

'Now you come to mention it,' said George, 'my contact said Oxford was on the stage or something – which is how comes he knows your—' I poked George in the side to shut him up. 'Hope!' George rubbed his side, 'I was going to say, that Oxford knows everybody.' A few minutes later George started whistling 'Rule Britannia'. 'Things might've just got a lot easier,' he said, when he'd finished his tune.

It weren't long before the sky started to get darker, and Henry was eager to find the place.

'W-we can always hide over the road or something,' he said. 'It's just it'll be hard to get our bearings if the area is in total darkness.'

We needn't have worried though. When we came into Lambeth Road, Bedlam shone out like Queen Vic's palace. It was massive and wasn't at all like I'd imagined.

'Bleeding 'ell,' said Jasper. 'If I could live there I'd murder me own brother, if I had one.'

'It's huge!' George spread his arms out wide as if trying to measure the length of the building. 'Where do we start?'

We hadn't really made an agreement, like. Everyone had their own bit of information: George had the keys and the contact; Henry thought he knew what this Oxford geezer might look like from a drawing in the paper. Jasper had the gift of the gab and said he'd easily wheedle his way pass the officers. But I didn't have anything much to give, except trying to keep the boys focused.

'When the lamps in the porch get lit, we'll climb over the side fence,' said George. He must've read my mind 'cause I was worried we wouldn't even get into the grounds. 'Everyone will be busy trying to give the inmates their dinners, and then get them into bed. I figure we have about an hour to find Oxford and get him to show us to Henry's ma's room.'

'Don't you think we'll be a little obvious? I mean, all four of us running around the place.' Henry looked worried. He'd come so far already; if we messed this up for him, Lord only knew what might happen. And it'd be back to Ma's place for me too!

George put his arm around Henry's shoulder to reassure him. 'We in't all goin' in, Henry. Jasper will get us through the first line of trouble. Then Hope will get us into the kitchens with them keys she has.'

'Then w-what?'

'Once we're in the building, you, being the only one that can read properly, will get into the doctor's office and find out where your ma is. If we can't find your ma, we'll find Oxford and he can show us the way.'

'And you? What are you doing, George?' I needed to know that if everything went pear-shaped, George and Jasper wouldn't just scarper, leaving me and Henry to take the rap.

'Me? I'll be nearby, keeping an eye on proceedings, won't I?'

'So…' I said. 'Once we've Henry's ma's records, or Oxford shows us where she is, we go in and rescue her, just like that?'

'Exactly.'

Well, it didn't quite turn out that way. Jasper got us past the officers, no trouble. But when we got to the kitchens, the door was not only locked but bolted too, from the inside.

'Now bleeding what?' We hadn't counted on no bolts.

'We try another door,' said Henry, as cool as anything. 'And we keep trying until we get in.'

We went around the building, trying doors, windows, even a cellar delivery hatch. Everything was locked down tight. The lights were still on inside, and when we got to the far side of the building we could hear a violin playing.

'Oxford!' Henry ran to the window. The curtains were drawn over, but there was a tiny gap where the curtains met. Henry pressed his face against the window.

'Can you see anything?' I asked.

'No, I think it's the dining room though. There seems to be a lot of movement.'

George was getting a bit jittery. 'Look, if I go around the front and make a distraction, maybe you can force a window or something?'

'I have your pa's knife Henry,' I said. 'I could slip it under the catch – that might work?'

'All right, but not here.' Henry looked along the row of windows. 'We need a window that's unlit.' Henry pointed along the building. 'There!'

So as George ran off in one direction, me and Henry headed towards the window a few yards away. Within minutes we heard shouting coming from the front of the asylum, and several lights appeared in the distance. Must've been the officers' lamps.

'This is it then.' Henry tried the window, but there was no movement. He tried it again, this time pulling the top sash downwards. Nothing.

'Here, let me.' I got the knife out of my satchel and pulled it from its sheath, the blade catching the light of a distant street lamp. Quickly, I slipped it between the two windows. 'It in't budging.'

'Let me try,' said Henry, taking the knife and jamming it in the gap between the panes. 'This is taking too long…'

A light came on in the room; someone must've entered. 'Shh,' I said, reaching out and holding Henry's hand still. Someone was heading towards the window – I could hear their footsteps getting closer.

'Quick!' I pulled Henry down, and we both squatted beneath the windowsill, crouching down. I could hear Henry breathing heavily – I put my finger to my lips and shushed him again. Henry sank to the ground and lay quietly waiting. The window opened a little and the smell of pipe tobacco drifted out.

'You see, Emma, travelling to Wales unaccompanied is out of the question.' A man's voice spoke calmly and clearly. 'I understand your predicament, and the urgency, but really you'll need to wait until your relative arrives to take you.'

Henry sat up and cowered at the opened window. 'Do you think…' he whispered, 'it could be my mother?'

I shrugged. 'Maybe.'

'W-what shall we do?' Henry whispered. 'This might be my chance.'

'I know,' I said. 'I'll tap the window, and if they look out, we might be able to see if it's her.'

Henry nodded. I picked up a couple of small stones from the ground and we ran and hid behind a small shrubbery, feet from the window.

'Right.' I threw the first stone at the window but it missed. The second hit it, but no one looked out.

'Throw it harder,' said Henry. 'Or let me...'

I stood up from behind the bush and threw as hard as I could. The stone clipped the stone ledge beneath the window loudly, and sure enough the curtains parted. An outline of two figures stood at the window, but I couldn't make out anything – other than it was a man and a woman – as the light behind them silhouetted their bodies.

'I can't see.' Henry moved forward slightly.

'Careful,' I said, holding onto Henry's shirt. 'They'll spot you.'

The shadowy figures moved away, but they left the curtains open.

'Now's our chance,' I said. 'Come on, we don't need no Oxford!'

# THE TRUTH – PART TWO

# 30

**Henry**

Hope beat me to the window, and was beckoning me to hurry up. When I got there I was confused – the view before me could've been a scene from a Vermeer painting. The man and woman were sitting in front of a small fire, even though it was May. The armchairs were angled towards the fireplace, their backs to the window, making it difficult for me to see their faces. A small table between them was set for high tea, a cake stand stacked with cakes, and the woman pouring the tea.

'W-what the…' I was speechless.

'Can you see if she looks like your mother, Henry?'

I was at a slightly better angle than Hope, but I could only see the side of the woman's face. 'I'm not sure – it could be. I mean… Hand me the sketchbook.' Hope pulled my father's sketchbook from her satchel and I opened it to reveal the images of my mother. 'The hair looks right. And the neck is…' It was no good, I was guessing, willing the woman to be my mother, when in fact she looked like any other woman. I sat down on the ground and dropped the sketchbook on my lap. 'I don't know…' That was all I could manage to say. Hope stayed watching through the window, waiting for the couple to leave so we could sneak in.

'W-what are they doing?' I asked.

'Nothing. Just sitting there.'

'Shall we try another window?' There was no point wasting time; everyone would be going to their rooms at any moment, then we'd be in real trouble. I picked up the sketchbook and studied the image of my mother. The picture must've been ten years old. And Father would've been drawing from memory. Maybe… I jumped up to look through the window again.

'What are you doin? Shh…' Hope pointed at the room beyond the open window. As I peered over the edge, the couple got up from their chairs.

'I'll send a messenger first thing tomorrow, Emma. I'll say you need to leave as soon as possible. I'm sure everything will be all right. You'll see.'

'Thank you, doctor.' The woman placed her napkin on the table and, as she turned towards the room, the lamplight illuminated her face.

'You know I would love to see my son, doctor. I just don't think I'm ready.'

I looked at Hope. It *was* my mother!

'Mo—' Hope cut me off, throwing me to the ground and holding her hand over my mouth. I fought like a mad thing, lashing out, kicking. Then George, appearing from nowhere, was on top of me, holding me down, whilst Hope pushed my face into the ground. I could feel my rage burning hot, about to burst out of me.

'What the Hell do you think you're doing?' I yelled when they finally released me. 'That's my mother in there.'

I leapt up at the window, but the room was empty. My mother was gone.

'Think, Henry,' said Hope. 'What if it in't your ma and you've blown our chances?'

'But it w-was, I'm positive.'

'Hope's right.' George sat down underneath the window. 'If we mess up now, you might never know the truth. Or find your ma.'

'B-but she was right there, you idiot.'

'And? Do you think even if it was your ma, she would know you?' Hope stood staring at me with her arms crossed. 'Well?'

'O-of course not, I was a baby… I…' As Hope moved away from the window I caught a glimpse of myself in the glass; she was right, what was there for my mother to recognise? I looked like some homeless vagrant – even *I* didn't recognise myself.

*

'We need proof, Henry. Real proof. And I bet we'll find it in there.' Hope pointed at the empty room.

'In you go then.' George cupped his hands together to give Hope a lift up. 'Henry?'

As Hope dropped through the window I stepped into George's hands and threw myself through after her. The scent of lily of the valley was overwhelming – Nana? Mother?

'I'll wait here,' said George. 'If anyone comes I'll whistle twice, like this…' George demonstrated his version of a nightingale, although it was an unlikely place to find one.

Hope headed straight for the desk in the centre of the room. She opened the drawers at random, quickly scanning the contents.

'There's nothing here.'

To the right of the fireplace was a tall mahogany cabinet, with drawers and cupboards beneath. I hurried across the room and tried the top drawer; it was locked. I rattled the cupboard doors; they were locked too.

'Hope, try the knife.'

Hope pulled my knife from her bag and pushed it between the drawer and the cabinet. After a few tries the drawer sprung free.

'This is it,' I said. 'Look, the doctor's patient casebooks...' I quickly rifled through the pile. But there wasn't one for a Lady Emma Mackenzie to be found. Hope opened the remaining drawers and cupboards; there were hundreds of casebooks, male patients filed on the left, female patients on the right-hand side of the cabinet. Hope found one for Edward Oxford and opened it to see what it said.

'Listen...' Hope stood bolt upright, holding her head at an angle and the casebook at arm's length. '"Edward Oxford, eighteen...to be D-E-T, det..."'

I took the casebook from her. '"To be detained at Her Majesties pleasure..." I thought you could read?'

'I can, but not proper. And fat chance I've got of practising with you around, and all.'

'W-we haven't got time to read Oxford's,' I said, putting the casebooks back in the cabinet. 'Now what? I'm sure that was Mother, but there aren't any documents to say one way or the other. I should've just called to her!'

Hope went to the tea table to help herself to some of the leftover cake. 'Waste not, want not,' she said, putting a whole slice of sponge cake in her mouth. 'Haann' on, looook,' she mumbled with her mouth full. Hope held up a single casebook that was on the floor, near the chair the man had been sitting in.

I snatched the document from her and read the name 'Miss Emma Hobbs', followed by her date of birth, and a diagnosis of her condition: '15th January 1820, Hysteric – with violent tendencies...' Some part of me was relieved that it couldn't be my mother after all. 'It's not her...'

Hope took the casebook and opened it. 'We need to be sure... If you says that the woman sitting in that chair...' Hope pointed to the armchair where my mother, or this Hobbs woman, had been sitting moments earlier. 'Was your ma, then this here book must give some light on the subject. If it in't, then it in't!'

'Didn't you hear me?' I yelled, feeling sure that woman was my mother. 'That's not her name!' I slapped the casebook out of Hope's hands and it fell to the floor.

'Henry!'

Hope bent down to pick the casebook up, and as she did so a sketch fell out onto the rug. It was a torn page from the *Illustrated London News*, showing the drawing of my mother.

## CLOSE ENCOUNTER

# 31

**Hope**

'Now what?' Henry was pretty certain that the woman we'd seen moments ago was his ma. After seeing the drawing, Henry was all but shocked into silence; I had to shake him to get him moving. 'Here – let's take the evidence, and think about what to do next. That doctor might be back any minute.'

George was at the window, waving frantically. 'Hurry up, you two. We in't got forever!'

Henry wanted to stay and talk to the doctor, but I was worried we might be arrested or locked away in the nuthouse ourselves. If the peelers were called, the least we'd be charged for was trespassing or breaking and entering. And Henry weren't convincing as no toff neither, so that weren't going to work.

After we tidied everything up, so as not to show we'd been there or nothing, Henry clambered back out through the window.

'I still think we should've w-waited,' he said, as he dropped to the ground. 'Here, pass me the casebook – I don't want it to get torn.' I leant through the window and passed Henry the book, then climbed through myself, careful to pull the curtains together and to leave the window as we found it.

'What now?' George was eager to get out of Bedlam as quickly as possible. 'Jasper will be wondering what's happening.'

'Maybe we should go back to the den? Then Henry can read his ma's notes and decide whether to come back or not.' I weren't sure how Henry would convince his ma or the doctor that he was her son; I'd done too good a job of disguising him.

'Right,' said George. 'Let's get moving then, before that bleeding officer does a patrol or something.'

'But the w-window is open,' said Henry. 'We might not get another chance to get in.'

'But there's no point in *getting in* when we don't know our next move, Henry.'

'Hope's right, Henry. If you stay and have it out with them, there's nothing to say they won't call the peelers or just throw us out.'

'B-but I'm sure I'd be able to convince my mother.' Henry looked back at the window; I couldn't imagine how he must be feeling inside. To be so close to meeting his mother after such a long time.

'Maybe Henry should try?' I couldn't believe what I was saying. But if it'd been my real pa, I knew nothing would've stopped me from speaking to him. 'If his ma don't believe him and it all goes wrong, you George, can cause another commotion to give us a chance of escape.'

Henry's face lit up. 'Really, Hope?'

'It's worth a try, like you said.'

George being George wasn't convinced. 'This in't going to end well; I can feel it in me bones.'

'Oh, shut up, George. You're beginning to sound like some old fortune teller.'

Henry laughed; he looked quite handsome when he wasn't carrying the weight of the world on his shoulders.

'Give us a hands up then, George.' And with that Henry slipped back through the window like an expert house-breaker.

Henry pulled me through after him.

'George, listen…' I said, leaning back out of the window. 'If we in't out within the hour, start making some uproar. And you'd better nip back and let Jasper know what's what, in case he gets twitchy.'

When we were back in the doctor's room, Henry decided he was just going to sit and wait. And when the doctor returned, Henry would ask him outright. So we sat by the fire, Henry choosing the armchair his ma had been sitting in.

'What do the notes say, Henry?'

'I'm frightened to look,' said Henry, opening the casebook and reading. 'I'm not sure I want to know all the details.'

Henry sat for ages, turning the pages, sighing every now and then, sometimes looking up from what he was reading, his face full of worry and sadness. 'It's too much,' he said, wiping his eyes on the back of his hand. 'It's so hard to believe… My mother, a common actress…'

'It weren't never going to be easy,' I said, taking a swig of cold tea. 'If you want to talk about it, I in't going to judge.'

'Thanks, Hope, but it's private. I'm not sure…'

I sat back in the armchair and waited for the drama to happen. I knew that if and when the doctor came back he wouldn't listen to me, or Henry. All he'd see was two thieves helping themselves to his tea and cake.

'Wait! Henry, I've an idea…' I put down the cup I was holding and opened my satchel. 'Look, your pa's sketchbook.' I held the blue book out to Henry. 'If you show this to the doctor, he'll have to believe you – it's got the sketches of your ma in it. And we've the letters…'

'I hadn't thought of that… That's if he gives us time to explain.'

Just as I was putting the sketchbook back in my satchel, the door opened and in walked the doctor. He must've been over six foot tall; he had dark, coal-black hair, and fancy sideburns. But what struck me most was the bright red cravat he was wearing – it reminded me of Mac's uniform, the one he'd put on to die.

'What the Hell is going on here?' The doctor turned to call out for help.

'Please, sir,' said Henry, leaping up from the armchair. 'I'm Henry William Mackenzie, son of the woman you were just having tea with.'

'Who? How did you get in my office?' The doctor strode into the room and pushed the door shut behind him.

All I could focus on was the doctor's red cravat. It seemed wrong somehow, such a cheerful colour in a place as cruel and desperate as Bedlam. And it made me think about Mac, lying dead in his uniform.

# THE 'MAD' DOCTOR

# 32

**Henry**

'Please, listen to me…' I held out my hand to shake the doctor's, but he ignored the gesture. 'I know it's hard to believe, sir, but it's true. I have proof—'

'Young man, I don't know what your game is, but we don't have anyone here by the name of Mackenzie.'

'That lady, the one that was sitting here.' Hope pointed to the armchair my mother had been sitting in. 'That lady, her name is Hobbs, in't it?'

'Excuse me? I'm not obliged to discuss my patients with you or anyone else.' The doctor walked over to the window and pulled back the curtains. 'I assume this is the way you came in? If you leave immediately, I shan't have reason to send for the authorities.' He stopped by his desk and started to go through his drawers, as if checking we hadn't taken anything.

'Are you my mother's doctor?' I held up the casebook and approached his desk. 'I know this says her name is Emma Hobbs, but her real name is Lady Emma Mackenzie. And she's my mother!' I stood with my arm outstretched, holding the evidence, but he didn't take it from me. I set the document down on the desk between us. 'If you'd just give me a few moments, I can explain. If you aren't convinced, I promise we will leave.'

'You have five minutes.' He took a pocket watch out of his inside jacket pocket and looked at it. It reminded me of Father's, the one I'd stupidly lost in the Thames.

'Your time starts now.'

Hope rushed forward and poured the contents of her satchel onto the desk. My father's compass and the sketchbook tumbled out, along with the bundle of letters, tied in green string.

'This is our proof, mister.' Hope picked up the sketchbook and opened it to a page with a picture of my mother. This here is Henry's ma. And there's no denying.'

'Sir, my father died in a miserable br-br... I mean, a house of ill repute.' I looked at Hope, suddenly aware that I was talking about her home. 'None of my father's family were with him. And this girl –' I pointed to Hope – 'was his only friend when he needed help. She's my only connection, and it's because of her I've been able to locate my mother... Who I thought was dead!'

The doctor looked at the remainder of my father's life spread out before him. 'I'm sorry, young man, but you could've picked these things up anywhere. That brothel for example, or even stolen them from some poor unsuspecting fellow.'

'But w-we didn't... I—'

'Why in't you letting Henry see his ma?' Hope jumped at the doctor like a feral cat, pushing him into the chair he was standing next to. 'Are you keeping her here against her will?'

'How dare you touch me?' The doctor leapt out of the chair, brushing his jacket lapels as if to wipe the experience from his person. Picking up the bundle of letters, he marched towards the door. 'I believe these belong to someone other than

156

156

yourselves. You have exactly one minute to leave before I call the officers.'

I tried to convince him again. 'If you were to fetch my mother I'm sure she'd recognise me, or something in me,' I said, trying to convince myself as much as the doctor. It was unlikely my mother would know me at all.

'Take a look at you,' said the doctor, waving his hand in my direction. 'Look at your clothes, and your scalped haircut. Do you really think that you're the son and heir of this imaginary Mackenzie family?' He smiled, almost sniggering to himself. 'If you do, you're obviously suffering from delusions of grandeur – a certifiable condition, I believe! Now leave—'

'Please!' I got down on my knees and begged the doctor. 'If you'll just speak to my m-mother…and—'

'Your time is up!' Taking a hand bell from a nearby shelf, the doctor opened the door and rang it loudly. 'Officer! Porter!' he called.

'Come on,' said Hope, pulling me up by my shirt. 'We're wasting our time.'

As I got up I felt as if my life had been shattered for the second time in as many days. My bones ached, and I didn't know what else to do, or where to go. No one believed me, and now the doctor had all our evidence too.

'Come on.' Hope tugged at me as if to wake me from the stupor I was in. 'If we in't out of here in a second, we'll be thrown in clink. Then what?'

As Hope started to put my father's belongings back in her satchel, the doctor rushed at us like a maniac. 'You can leave those too; they don't belong to you!' He swiped at Hope, but she was quicker. Scooping the rest of the things into her bag, she dodged under the doctor's arms and out of the window, grabbing Mother's casebook as she went by. 'You stop there,' he said, pointing at me. 'We'll see what the police constable has to say about this.' He put my father's letters down on his desk and took hold of me.

Hope appeared at the window. 'Henry, run!'

Before I realised what I was doing, I kicked the doctor hard and he buckled. As he did so I pushed him to the ground, snatched the letters from his desk and leapt out of the window too.

# RETURN TO JACOB'S

# 33

**Henry**

The journey back to Jacob's Island was awful. George, Jasper and Hope all thought they'd let me down. Bedlam would now have its security increased, so there was absolutely no chance of getting into the place again. No one spoke as we shuffled back across London; the smog had descended thicker than usual, so it was hard to even see my friends. I didn't know what to do next. Should I just go home and explain to Nana? I wasn't sure I could remain calm if I thought Nana had known all along about my mother, but I had to think about Nana's illness; this could finish her off and I didn't want to be responsible for upsetting her and making her worse.

I could confront Xavier – he surely couldn't deny he had written the letters, so one way or another he knew about my father and his condition. And probably my mother too. Xavier was responsible for this turmoil!

'Henry?' Hope's voice was faint and gentle coming at me through the dense fog. 'Are you all right?' Her hand reached out and touched mine. 'We'll sort it, won't we, boys?'

George and Jasper closed in, and put their arms around my shoulders. 'Course we will,' said George. 'After all, Jasper here says he knows this Xavier geezer. Don't you, Jasper?'

'I said all along, he's only trying to help.' Jasper let go of me and moved away. 'But no one listens to old Jasper, do they?'

When we got to Jacob's Island our mood was heavy. Crooner and Tosher were waiting for us by the footbridge I'd slipped on earlier. I'd almost forgotten about them.

'You can't stay here,' Tosher said. 'The peelers have been swarming the place since you left.'

The dim light of a tavern's lamp pooled at our feet. 'Where's Jasper?' asked Crooner. We all looked around, straining to see further than the length of our arms.

'Jasper?' Hope called into the smog. 'Jasper!'

'Stop messing about!' shouted George, cupping his hands to make his voice travel further.

There was no answer – Jasper had simply disappeared into the night, with not a word about where he was going.

# Going Home

# 34

**Hope**

'I'll kill the bleeding git if he's double-crossed us, I swear I will.' I knew Jasper couldn't be trusted; I just had that feeling. And I was an idiot letting him be part of our plans – I should've listened to the boys.

'Well, now what?' asked Tosher. 'We've been running and hiding all day; them peelers don't give up.'

'I'll go home,' said Henry. 'There's nothing else we can do. Maybe Mrs Banks can sort things out.'

'Who the bleeding 'ell is Mrs Banks? We don't need no grown-ups.' George had real suspicions of adults, and I didn't blame him, not with the life he'd had. He weren't one to give up neither, and he definitely didn't like to admit to failure.

'Henry's housekeeper! In't it, Henry?'

'Yes, well, more than that really – she's part of our family, and she's always been there for me.'

'Stuff the housekeeper, or whatever. We'll find Jasper and wring his bleeding neck. Then we'll get that uncle of yours to cough for his crimes.' George was waving his arms about frantically as if, by gesturing, everything would suddenly fall into place.

'George, that in't going to happen; Jasper will be long gone.' I was angry with myself for not helping Henry free his mother from the madhouse. But what really hurt me was the thought of Mac having put so much trust in me, and I'd let him down. I didn't want Henry to go home neither; he'd become a real friend to me and I'd miss him. I looked at the four boys huddled together in the yellow gaslight; Henry could easily pass for one of them, but he'd his own life to lead – a much better life than ours.

'Listen,' I said, breaking the silence, 'if we don't move soon we'll all be for the chop.'

'So,' said George, 'if Henry needs to go home, that's fine. But we in't giving up yet.'

Crooner put his arm around Henry's shoulders. 'We'll get your ma, Henry, you'll see. You best get back to your nana.' Crooner, who never spoke!

'How are we going to get Henry here back to… Where is it you live?' said George.

'Belgravia.' Henry went quiet, as if he was thinking about his life before his world came crashing down on him. 'You can see a large oak tree in the garden from my bedroom window. I had a treehouse in it when I was little.'

We all stood in silence, imagining Henry's treehouse and the view from his window. What a life he had – to eat when not even hungry, to sleep in a real bed, and to be warm on a winter's night. Henry's life was so different from ours. It would be hard for him, learning to live with no parents, but for us – 'specially the boys – living without no tree house weren't nothing to worry about.

'We've some money left.' I dug deep into my satchel and brought out the remaining coins. 'You could get a cab, and be home in no time.'

'What about you? What will you all do?' Henry looked at us all in turn – me, George, Crooner and Tosher.

'Don't you worry about us,' said George. 'We does all right, don't we, boys?'

'Yeah, course,' said the twins together.

'Thank you for trying to help me. I'll never forget you and w-what you risked.' Henry looked as if he might start blubbering, but he held it together. 'W-when I'm able, I'll come and find you, all of you, and we'll eat a whole pig, not just sausages.'

'Course you will,' said Tosher. 'And we'll all ride in your grandma's carriage, out in the countryside like Queen Victoria, God bless her soul.' Tosher laughed and shoved Crooner in the ribs, which made him start coughing and choking. 'We'll see you around then, eh? Come on, George.'

The three boys ran off across the footbridge and faded into the night-time. Henry looked around as if trying to remember why or how he'd ever ended up on Jacob's Island.

'In some w-ways, I'll miss this place,' he said.

'Give over, there in't nothing worth missing here.' Although I hoped Henry would miss me, at least a little. I would definitely miss him. 'Here, I'll walk you to London Bridge; you'll never get a cab from here.'

'Thank you, Hope.' Henry turned towards me and held my hands tightly. 'You know, I w-will come back,' he said. Then, letting go of my hands, he took off his cap and placed it on my head. 'I'll speak to my nana and get her to take me to Bethlem, or should I say Bedlam? It'll work out in the end, I'm sure of it.' Henry rubbed at his crazy shorn red hair. 'That's if she recognises me.'

'All right, Henry,' I said, trying to hold back the tears. But I didn't believe him, not really, and even if he did come back, I'd be long gone – after all I had Pa to worry about.

# CRAZINESS

# 35

**Henry**

By the time we got to the bridge it was well and truly dark. I'd never been out on the streets before, not like this anyway. There were fewer hansom cabs around, but plenty more people, particularly women of a certain persuasion. Hope looped her arm through mine and held on tight.

'Best they think we're together,' she said.

'Why? Surely they won't be interested in a penniless vagrant.' We both laughed at the absurdity of my situation. Here I was, one of the wealthiest young men in London, and I probably wouldn't even be able to get a cab.

'Here, you better have this.' Hope handed me her satchel. 'You might need it to prove about your ma an' all.'

'Thank you.' I put the satchel over my shoulder, the way I'd seen Hope do. The contents would be safer that way. 'Hope, w-what you've sacrificed for me, I'll never forget, never.'

Hope threw her arms around me and kissed me on the cheek. 'Sorry,' she said, pulling away. 'I didn't mean to… It's just… For God's sake, get out of here.' Hope gave me a shove, which I now knew was a sign of affection. Taking her in my arms, I held her as tight as I could; I didn't want to let go. Hope had become a best friend to me – more than that…

'Why don't you come with me?' I said.

'Can you imagine?' When Hope smiled her whole face lit up. 'No, Henry, that just in't possible, not even for you.'

'But…'

'No, Henry. Please don't…'

I put out my hand and waved down a cab. 'I *will* be back, once this is sorted, you can be sure of that.'

As the cab came to a halt, I opened the door and climbed in, then leant out of the window and waved. 'Goodbye, Hope. Thank you – for everything.'

As I sat down I realised there was someone else in the cab. 'Oh, I'm sorry, sir. I didn't realise the cab was occup—'

Leaning forward the man said, 'That's all right, Henry. I believe we're going the same way.'

'Xavier? What? How?' I tried to open the door to get out, but he held onto the handle. 'But, Hope?'

I shouted out of the window into the darkness, 'Hoooope!' But there was no reply.

'Henry, sit down! Shouting out of the window is unbecoming of a gentleman.' Xavier sat back and relaxed, taking his hand off the door. 'I believe you have something belonging to me?' He held out his hand, waiting for me to hand him the satchel.

'It's not yours,' I said defiantly. 'This bag belongs to Hope.'

'And the contents…belong to me.' Xavier leant across me to take the satchel.

'The contents…belong…to me! My father left his things for me, not you.' I held on tight to the satchel, gripping it with every ounce of strength I had.

'Have it your way.' Xavier leant back into his seat. 'Your grandmother is sick, very sick, Henry. That drama at the Great

Exhibition, and then running away as you did – it's all been too much.'

'It's all your fault,' I said. 'You knew Father was at that place, but you did nothing to help him. And my mother... What about her?'

'What it is to be ignorant of life's many deceptions, Henry.'

'I don't care w-what you say. I know you're involved in this somehow. And I'll prove it. N-Nana will believe me.'

Xavier remained silent for the rest of the journey home. I thought about beating him with Hope's bag and jumping out of the moving cab. At least I knew where I was with the boys and Hope. But Nana would want to see me, and I couldn't cope with the thought that she might die before I got to speak to her and explain. And for once hear the truth.

*

The lights were all on when we arrived home; even the old servants' rooms were lit up like a Christmas tree. As I entered the hallway Mrs Banks rushed to my side. 'Where have you been? We've been out of our minds with worry.' Taking the satchel off me, and practically stripping me of my clothes, she said, 'Lord above, what's happened to you, lad? Seeing you like this will finish your nana off!' Mrs Banks handed me a gown and slippers. 'Be prepared, Henry. And try to be brave, child.'

'I'm not a child, Mrs Banks, I can deal with it.' I raced up the stairs to Nana's bedroom.

Nana was propped up on several pillows, the blankets tucked up under her chin as if it were the middle of winter. The fire blazed in the hearth and the curtains were drawn tightly shut. I sat down on the side of Nana's bed and felt for her hand under the eiderdown; her fingers were like icicles.

'Henry?'

'I'm here, Nana.'

Opening her eyes a little, Nana tried to smile. 'Where have you been?'

I couldn't tell Nana the truth, but I didn't want to lie either – there had been enough lies. 'Xavier, I mean, Uncle Xavier, has brought me home,' I said quietly.

'That's good. I'm pleased you're back.'

I sat on the side of Nana's bed for ages, wondering how I could ask her about Mother without upsetting her too much. But Nana kept falling asleep, so sometimes when I spoke she didn't respond. And other times when I thought she was asleep she'd suddenly grab my hand, or call out, 'Henry!' I didn't know whether she was calling for my father, or me, but it didn't really matter. As the grandfather clock struck eleven, Mrs Banks came into the bedroom and told me she'd prepared a bath.

'When you're all washed, come down to the kitchen; I've prepared some hot cocoa and buns.'

I hadn't eaten for hours, and my stomach ached as though I'd been starved for a week. But I thought about Hope, George, Tosher and Crooner scraping around for stale bread, and stealing to keep their hunger at bay. 'I'm not hungry, thank you, Mrs Banks, but I'd like to see my uncle before he retires.'

'If you say so, Henry. I'll let him know when I go downstairs.'

*

Xavier was waiting in the drawing room. Hope's satchel was on the sideboard; it appeared the contents were still intact. I looked at my uncle and then at the satchel. 'I suppose you've been through Hope's bag and taken any incriminating evidence?'

**167**

'Sit down, Henry.' Xavier motioned to the armchair opposite his. 'I know what you think, Henry. But I can assure you everything I did was to protect you.'

'How? By letting Father die in that f-filthy b-brothel? And hiding my mother away in that…that a-asylum?'

'Henry, you've obviously made up your mind about me. And I don't blame you. I would've come to the same conclusion myself at your age. I admit I have my faults—'

'This isn't about my age! It's about you, and it's about Nana.' I didn't know how to string it all together, and everything just came tumbling out. 'I thought Mother was dead. You all lied to me. And when Father came back you kept him from me…' The anger and frustration was pulsing through my veins. 'Damn it, I'm fifteen years old – I'm old enough to understand.'

'Yes, you are now. A week ago you were still an innocent child.' Xavier handed me a letter, which looked like one of the ones Father had written to me. 'Read this.'

I snatched the letter from him. 'You've been through…' Then I read the envelope:

*(Personal Correspondence – Strictly Private)*
*Sir Xavier Barrington Mackenzie*
*c/o The Oriental*
*London*

'This is addressed to you? But it's my father's handwriting…?'

'Yes, Henry.' Xavier went to the sideboard, picked up Hope's satchel and handed it to me. 'I'll leave you to read the letter alone. And if you want to know the whole truth, I suggest you read your mother's case notes thoroughly.'

# Xavier's Letter

# 36

**Henry**

When my uncle had left the room I took the letter from the envelope, afraid of what I might discover. It was dated 27th April 1851… The same date as the letter my father gave to Hope. I read on…

*27th April 1851*
*Cable Street*
*Whitechapel*

*Dear Xavier,*

*I know we haven't always seen eye to eye, particularly with regard to my enlisting in the military, instead of following you into the East India Co. – so I appreciated your visit Monday last, and your assured discretion.*

*As I explained in my previous correspondence, my condition is hopeless and I fear I only have a short time left. I need you to carry out my request and protect my son Henry at all costs. The tyrant that rules this place may try to discredit or blackmail the family – he knows about the opium, and your gambling. God knows what else he knows.*

*I believe he may have taken some of the letters I wrote to my son too; my darling boy. You must secure them by any means possible – I don't want Henry involved.*

*There is a young girl here who has been caring for me; her name is Hope. I've asked her to take my belongings to Henry should I die before you come. But she is vulnerable, and that brute of a father may force her to woo Henry – the man has no scruples. Keep an eye on her, brother; when I'm gone, who knows what she may be forced to do.*

*Thank you for offering to take me to a convalescent hospice, and I will ready myself. All I ask is that you keep my identity and whereabouts anonymous; Mother lost her son in '42 – let it remain that way.*

*If what you say about Emma is correct, then, as much as it pains me to say, it is probably better for her health, and Henry's welfare, that she remains at Bethlem. If, however, Henry should find out about his mother's condition and her location, please move her – seeing her son as a young man may well set her progress back years.*

*Should this letter be my last to you, Xavier, please care for my son as though he were your own.*

*With infinite appreciation.*

*Your brother, Henry William Mackenzie*

I read the letter again. Father did know about Mother? *And,* he *chose* not to contact or see me! I couldn't take it in – everything I'd thought about Xavier, and about my father, was wrong. I pulled Mother's case notes from Hope's satchel and read the paragraph I couldn't face reading before: Mother's diagnosis.

*After receiving news that the army in Afghanistan were wiped out in January 1842 with only one survivor, the patient, Lady Emma Mackenzie (herein known as Miss Emma Hobbs), having gone into uncontrollable hysterics, was removed from her home for the safety of her son – a young child named Henry... Diagnosis: 'hysteric with manic tendencies'.*

Removed for my safety? I rang the bell that hung down the side of the fireplace. Xavier appeared moments later with Mrs Banks. I held out the casebook.

'Why? Surely Mother must be well by now?' I was in shock. I sat down in the armchair, trying to understand the madness that had destroyed my family. 'You could've explained... I went to that filthy place, and had to live in... My suit... I nearly drowned... Hope! And all the time you both knew?'

'Oh, Henry.' Mrs Banks rushed to hug me, but I pushed her away.

'No. Not this time.'

'I'm sorry, Henry.' Uncle Xavier sat down in the chair opposite me. 'I was in Paris when your father died. I hadn't told anyone about his condition or whereabouts, at his request. When I came back, your nana told me about the newspaper article. I thought it best to send you away to school until the mess was sorted, but your nana was against it. And you – you had other ideas...'

'You could've cared for Mother here surely?' I looked at Mrs Banks. 'You could've got help in?'

'Henry, try to understand,' said Mrs Banks, reaching out to touch me. 'Your poor mother was out of her mind – she... Well, I don't like to say... She—'

'She what?' I shouted. All this avoiding the truth, keeping secrets and lying was making me so frustrated. 'She what?'

Xavier leant across and held my hand. 'Henry, your mother lost control of her mind when she heard that the whole regiment

**171**

had been killed. She ran around the house, screaming, crying, smashing things...' Xavier looked at Mrs Banks, who nodded for him to continue. 'We think it was an accident, but your mother pushed you out of her way and you fell down the stairs... We thought you were dead...'

'I don't believe you.' I tried to think back, but I couldn't remember my mother at all; I could hear music, a piano playing. But no picture came to mind.

'It's true, Henry.' Mrs Banks touched my head where I'd been scratching since having my hair cut. 'Here, this is where you cut your head open. Bled like anything, you did.' I felt the place Mrs Banks had touched; there was a long, raised scar. 'You'd just started talking in proper sentences too,' she said. 'But after that you didn't speak, not for years.'

It all began to make sense. My stammer, the nightmares, and the fact I'd always been allowed to grow my hair long, even though Nana's lady friends said it should be cut. Even Uncle Xavier's timely appearances in Whitechapel, and Jasper...

'Did Jasper report back to you?'

'He was paid to keep close – you were acting in such a strange way, we were worried,' said Xavier. 'But I think he took a liking to you. He gave me this...' Xavier felt in his pocket and brought out a pocket watch. 'Jasper returned to the river and searched for hours until he found it...'

'Father's watch!'

'I had it cleaned and repaired. Jasper's a good boy, Henry.'

Tears began to burn my eyes. 'And Hope? Is she good? Or was she paid too?'

'Hope? The daughter of that thieving scoundrel? She was part of their plan, Henry. A con woman in the making! Surely you see that?'

'You're lying! I know it! Hope saved my life.'

172

'I think you'll find that Jasper saved your life, Henry. Think—'

'I don't believe you. I want to find her – what have you done with her?'

'I haven't done anything with her. But the law will decide whether she is as innocent as you suggest.'

Before I could answer, there was a gentle knock on the drawing room door. I looked at Mrs Banks. 'Who's that?'

'We brought in a nurse to sit with your nana…' Mrs Banks went to the door. The person spoke quietly, whispering to Mrs Banks. I strained my ears to hear, but all I heard was a low murmuring. When Mrs Banks turned back to the room her face was colourless. 'Your nana, Her Ladyship… I'm afraid she's gone…'

# THE OLD BAILEY

# 37

*23rd June 1851*

**Hope**

After Henry got into the cab, two bleeding peelers grabbed me from behind. 'Right, you little madam, we've got your card, we 'ave.' I tried to get away but they shackled me and threw me in the Black Maria. The peelers found Henry's knife on me, and said it was evidence. I'd forgotten it was in my belt.

I waited for Henry to come and prove me innocent. But he didn't. Even the boys stayed away until my sentencing.

'Your ma and pa have disappeared, leaving no trace,' said George through the cell door. 'We can't get near to Henry's house neither – bluebottles everywhere. And the windows are all shut up.'

'What about Aunt Sal?' I said. 'She saw Henry. Or...or Jasper. He knows the truth.'

'The Beak won't listen to nobody.'

George was right. I knew it deep down; since when had my sort had a voice? Maybe this was God punishing me for not speaking up about Mac!

'There's a bit of a commotion upstairs,' said George, pointing up to the waiting courtroom. 'Some social reformer is arguing your case.'

'Do you think the Beak will listen?'

'Who knows? I'll go back up, and if I hear anything I'll come straight down again.' George slipped off, and I watched as he raced past my tiny cell window.

George had only been gone a few moments when one of the court officers arrived, clanking his keys. 'Right, here we go.' He opened the cell door and put on the handcuffs. 'No funny business, right!'

As I walked to the courtroom, I thought about the last few weeks. If it hadn't been for Henry, I would've taken my place as one of Ma's girls – Pa's prized possession – or have been sent to the colonies as some old crone's wife. But I'd rather this death than living that life... I was glad in a way that Henry had come to Whitechapel. We'd had some near escapes, but I felt as though I'd tried to pay my debt to Mac. And Henry? Well, I'd got to like his odd ways – he made me smile.

With any luck, when I was gone, George would find my ma and sisters and get to Henry for help. But for now...

# THE HANGING JUDGE

# 38

**Henry**

The courtroom was packed. It seemed as though everyone from Whitechapel to Jacob's Island had come to object to Hope's sentencing. Xavier had suggested we wait in the barouche until things had settled down. But I wanted Hope to know I was there, and that I hadn't forgotten her. Even though Xavier didn't trust her, I persuaded him to allow me to attend the court hearing. I understood Xavier's concern, especially after Mrs Banks said that Nana was worried 'the girl' might try to manipulate me somehow – and history might repeat itself. That was why Xavier had sent Jasper to watch me. They obviously didn't know Hope.

It was difficult to get near the front of the court, even with Mrs Banks shoving people in their ribs. I could see George peering through the rails of the upper floor, and Tosher and Crooner were squashed near the rear window.

'The court will stand…' Everyone shuffled and pushed. 'The Right Honourable Judge Jeffreys.'

The judge sat down, and the courtroom followed – though there wasn't much room for people to stand, let alone sit.

'The sentencing of Hope Isaacs will be revoked. Instead, she will be sentenced to fifteen years in the colonies.'

Everyone gasped. George shouted out, 'Liars! You're all bleedin' liars! Hope in't done nothin'!'

'You call this justice?' Crooner shouted from the back of the courtroom. Crooner, who rarely spoke a word! Everyone started shouting at the same time. I tried to push to the front – if only I could get to speak.

'P-please, let me through…' I slipped under a nursing mother's arms. 'Please, I need to speak to the judge…'

A huge man with arms like tree trunks made a gap in the crowd. 'Let the lad through.' The rabble closed around me; I looked to see if Xavier and Mrs Banks were anywhere nearby, but they'd been swallowed by the masses – I was on my own!

'I said, let him through.' The giant pushed through the crowd, making a human barrier. Everyone in the courthouse was shouting, crying or banging on the walls and floors. I could see Hope and the judge.

'Hope!' I shouted above the noise. 'Hope!' I couldn't let this happen… 'Hope, it's me, Henry!'

The judge raised his hand. 'Order, order…' He banged his fist down hard on the mahogany surface. 'Order, I say.'

As the court went quiet I squeezed to the front and addressed the judge. 'Sir, this young lady is innocent. I can vouch for her myself.'

'And who are you?'

The crowd went silent. 'I'm H-Henry W-William Mackenzie, grandson of the late Lady Eveline Mackenzie, son and heir of the late Lord Henry Mackenzie, *and* the so-called *victim* in this case.'

Hope looked terrified; I'd never seen her scared before. I wanted to protect her from this aged old fool who couldn't see further than his nose.

'Y-Your Honour,' I said. 'I believe if...if there are no charges, there can be no case?'

'Well...' The judge mumbled to one of the officers, 'But I've already passed sentence.'

'You can't sentence someone if there isn't a crime,' I said. 'Please!'

More mumbling. I looked at Hope and she smiled, the radiance in her face returning.

'We have the evidence,' said Judge Jeffreys, holding up Father's knife. 'It was found on the girl...'

'Hope was l-looking after it for me, at my request,' I said. Why hadn't I thought about the knife when I emptied Hope's satchel?

The judge whispered something to a court official. 'Court adjourned. Session will resume after lunch.'

The policemen grabbed hold of Hope and she disappeared below dock.

'Hope...' I called. 'It'll be all right. I promise.'

Hope's voice echoed up the court stairs. 'Henry – Lily, Rose – promise...'

'I promise...' But I don't think she heard me.

I tried to see Hope in the cells, but no amount of bribery gained me entry. I went back to the courtroom. It was hours before the judge returned.

*

As the old fool entered the courtroom, George was waving at me and giving me the thumbs up. Xavier and Mrs Banks appeared on the balcony of the courtroom. The judge whispered to the official – who wrote something in his book. Suddenly my uncle began clapping and jeering, and Mrs Banks joined him, shouting, 'Let her go! Let her go!' Then the whole courtroom went into an uproar. Hope was still standing in the dock; I could see her shaking, tears streaming down her face. As I tried to reach her to comfort her, the judge banged his fist down hard on his counter again.

'Silence in the courtroom!' shouted the court official over the noise.

Everyone went quiet.

The judge stood up and waited for the last few children to be silent.

'Case dismissed!' he said. 'Miss, you're free to leave.'

# The Final Scene

# 39

**Hope**

So there was another ending. Henry came through, just as he said he would – just as Mac promised.

After my trial, Henry, George, Crooner, Tosher and even that two-face Jasper came with us for a slap-up dinner at the Olde Cheshire Cheese. The twins ate that much I swore they were as round as George by the time they'd finished. After dinner, we all went for a long ride out to the countryside in Henry's grandma's barouche, where we stopped for a picnic by a stream.

Henry offered apprenticeships to the boys, on his estate in Scotland. But only Jasper said yes. George and the twins said they preferred their freedom, and couldn't live anywhere else but London. 'But,' said George, 'a hot dinner and a soft bed once in a while wouldn't be missed.'

'And a hot bath,' Henry added.

That night was the happiest night I'd had in a long time, and I didn't want it to end. But eventually it did.

\*

'So,' said Henry, after the boys had left, 'I was wondering if you'd like to come and work at my home?'

'Work? At your home?' I said. 'What as? A maid-of-all-works?' I weren't sure I'd like being trapped in a house all day neither. Like the boys said, there was a lot to be said for roaming free.

'No. I thought you might like to be my mother's companion, while you train to be a nurse.' Henry smiled.

'Your mother? I thought she'd—'

'She's coming home, Hope.' Henry's face flushed with joy. 'I thought Mother could help you with your reading and writing too.'

'That's wonderful news. I'm so happy for you, Henry.' And I genuinely was. But it only made the loss of my ma and sisters even more painful.

'And before you say anything else, I've hired a private investigator to find your family. And once he does, there will be a home and a livelihood waiting for them too. And a hangman's noose for that beast of a man – your step-pa. It seems you were right about Father being murdered. Xavier found out that your step-pa had spent the money he'd given to your ma for her silence on strychnine.'

'Henry…I…I feel so ashamed.'

'It's not your fault, Hope.' Henry held me close. 'I want you with me, always. You're my best friend.'

'Henry, I don't know what to say.'

'Well, that'll be a first!'

# Acknowledgements

To my critique partners at Bath Spa University whose early input to this novel was essential to its development – as well as my own as a writer – Rowena House, Lucy Van Smit, Chris Vick, Eden Endfield, Sarah Henderson, Irulan Horner and Philippa Forrester. To my fellow writers who have read and commented on various drafts of Restless: A Novella – Julia (J. M. Forster), Sharon Tregenza and Eugene Lambert.

To my husband Leigh who has had to put up with me in writer mode for the last few years. To my children who have supported and encouraged me every step of the way – Lester, Emma, Amy & Joccoaa.

Finally, I'd like to thank Rachel Lawston for her beautiful cover design and text layout, and Catherine Coe for her close copy editing skills.

If you or a family member has been affected by the issues touched on in the novel, please seek support via:

**(PTSD) Post Traumatic Stress Disorder**
http://www.mind.org.uk
https://www.helpforheroes.org.uk/get-support/

**Drug/Alcohol Misuse or addiction**
http://www.turning-point.co.uk

**Sexual Exploitation**
http://beyondthestreets.org.uk

Lightning Source UK Ltd.
Milton Keynes UK
UKHW012009101220
374921UK00004B/1233